C000228485

The Boy

WYTSKE VERSTEEG is a Dutch author and political scientist. In 2008 Versteeg published *This is Not a Homeless Person* (*Dit is geen dakloze*) about her experiences as a volunteer, mixing philosophical literature with journalistic observations and personal accounts of homelessness. Her debut novel *Weightless* (*De wezenlozen*) was nominated for the 2013 Opzij Literature Prize and longlisted for the AKO Literature Prize. *The Boy* is Versteeg's second novel; it has been translated into German, Italian, Turkish and Danish. It won the 2014 BNG Bank Literature Prize and was longlisted for the prestigious Libris Literature Prize.

The Boy

WYTSKE VERSTEEG

Translated from the Dutch
by Sarah Welling

hoperoad : London

HopeRoad Publishing Ltd
P O Box 55544
Exhibition Road
London SW7 2DB

First published in Great Britain by HopeRoad 2016

Original Dutch edition first published in 2013
BOY Wytske Versteeg

Copyright © 2013 Wytske Versteeg

English translation Copyright © Sarah Welling 2016

The rights of Wytske Versteeg and Sarah Welling to be identified as the
author and translator of this work respectively have been asserted by them
in accordance with the Copyright, Designs and Patents Act 1988

A catalogue for this book is available from the British Library

All rights reserved. No part of this book may be
reproduced, stored in a retrieval system or transmitted
in any form or by any means, electronic, mechanical,
photocopying, recording or otherwise, without the
prior permission of the publishers.

This book is sold subject to the condition that it shall not,
by way of trade or otherwise, be lent, re-sold, hired out or otherwise
circulated without the publisher's prior consent in any form of
binding or cover other than that in which it is published and
without a similar condition including the condition being
imposed on the subsequent purchaser.

This book was published with the support of the Dutch
Foundation for Literature

ISBN 978-1-908446-50-3
eISBN 978-1-908446-55-8

Printed and bound by TJ International Ltd, Padstow, Cornwall, UK

www.hoperoadpublishing.com

I

THE BODY ALWAYS surfaces, that's how the woman put it. 'People think it's easy, that they can just disappear.'

Her name was Joyce and she wore sack-like dresses in a dark shade of purple. She'd been showing up at my house all too often the past few weeks. You don't send the police away; you offer them coffee instead. And when they come round more often than you'd like, you try to hide it, even if that takes an effort. Because they're the only ones who still have the power to help you. So you buy an apple pie, as if that will make a difference, as if a piece of pie is going to make them widen their search, intensify it. You welcome them with a convincing show of warmth.

It was too late for that now – I saw it in their faces when I opened the door, and yet I still let them in. There's a protocol for these kinds of things; they must practise for situations like this.

The tone of her voice wasn't right.

They had come here to say the sentence I didn't want to hear. I'd have to press my hands to my ears, start singing very loudly. I'd have to make a sound, any sound, as long as it was loud enough to drown out her message, to undo it.

'They think, I'm ending it and that'll be it. But the body always turns up.'

3

'We're very sorry,' her partner interrupted. His name was Walter. He had a habit of hooking his thumbs behind the waistband of his jeans, like a cowboy in a second-rate film. I wondered if he watched a lot of crime shows and took his cues from them; he had a slightly embittered air that didn't entirely suit him.

I offered them something to drink and they declined politely. I got up and made them tea anyway. They thanked me, but never even touched the mugs.

They still hadn't said his name, which meant all this could still be about someone else, about some other body. They asked me if I wanted to call Mark and I told them he'd been in Nairobi for the past few days. 'He's there quite often for work.'

They weren't interested, but I wanted to keep the conversation going, to keep talking about something else. I said Mark would be flying back just about now, and I wouldn't be able to get through to him.

Was there anyone else, then – should they send someone to the airport, maybe? A note of pity had crept into the female officer's voice.

'I'll manage,' I said, 'thank you.'

I refused to play along and act like we were friends; refused, too, to pretend that the past few months had not taken place. Walter cleared his throat. 'It won't seem possible to you now, but often it's better in the end, to know that someone has passed away, better than them remaining missing.'

'His name is Kito,' I said.

'In the end, there's a kind of closure, once you know someone has died. Not really, not completely, but you can find a kind of peace. No need to keep hoping.'

4

'Life goes on,' I said cynically, and this time it was the woman who interrupted him and said that, again, they were very sorry and I could call anytime.

I walked them to the door. It was only after I had closed it behind them – calmly, in control – that I collapsed into a heap on the floor, my knees drawn up, my arms clasping them tight, leaning against the door as if I could still keep the evil out.

The dead always come to the surface. Maybe that's why we cover them with slabs of marble, gleaming but heavy, doors never to be opened again. That's what the rituals are for. It's why we put make-up on the deceased to make them look like their old selves, with a bit of rouge on their cheeks and in their best clothes. Why we send hand-written cards to everyone, informing them of our loss. We ask all our loved ones to be by our side when the coffin is lowered into the earth or disappears from sight, to be with us when we say goodbye. No matter how old or distant the deceased, we always think of ourselves and how little time we have left, and that's why we laugh too loudly and order coffee and cake, because as long as we are eating we are alive. But when a child dies, nobody feels like eating, and guests slip away as soon as the service is over. Nobody dares say how lovely, how peaceful he looked.

Not that that there was any question of that. Kito was buried in a closed coffin. He'd been missing too long.

'Can I see him?' I had asked. Suddenly that was the only thing I wanted.

The woman cleared her throat. 'You need to understand that the water' – I was already reaching for my coat – 'the length of time Kito spent in the water, in our climate – that he's not there anymore, not the way you knew him.'

That his skin was gone – that was what she meant – that his skin, muscles and fat were gone, that his face had slipped from his skull.

My son's washed-up body was found by someone out walking their dog. Sometimes I try to picture how it happened: whether it was a woman who found him, and what kind of dog it was, and how they were walking along, the two of them, their feet sinking into the sand. I see a small, overweight woman, grey-haired and wearing a duffel coat, because it was cold on the beach. The way I imagine it, the dog wasn't the small, yappy kind that would run off with a bone, but a German Shepherd perhaps, a loyal animal that stopped when he came up to Kito and barked to alert his owner. I imagine her taking off the large shawl she was wearing and using it to cover Kito even before she called the police. I hope she didn't just recoil as you might well do when finding a corpse. (A word nobody mentions, not even you, and everyone, including the undertaker, carefully avoids, until you get sick of all the euphemisms and the way people tiptoe around. Which may also be because the jokes you make now are of the blackest kind and they don't understand that, they don't realize that there's no other way.)

I wasn't worried the day Kito didn't come home. I didn't have a premonition, nothing to tell me something was wrong. Maybe I was whistling a tune when he was already dead. Maybe I was thinking about our plans for the weekend or next week. Or of my appointments, neatly lined up back to back, and the holidays that were coming up.

When was the first time I looked at my watch?

I had my appointments. I listened to my patients, who put their lives out on display for me and hoped I could cure them by giving them a pill. I said they needed to take responsibility. I gave them a firm handshake when they came in and weren't able to meet my eye. I put some warmth in my voice, which made them warm to me. They knew my time was valuable and they looked up to me, thinking I had some kind of power they didn't, or at least access to the drugs they needed. I told them they could influence their thoughts. They summed up their symptoms one by one: the insomnia, the restless legs, the mental fog that wouldn't lift. I wrote prescriptions and read files. Maybe by that time the water was already tugging at my child. I called an insurance firm, not an ambulance, and I didn't call for help.

I want to shake her, the woman I used to be, and tell her to go to the beach, now, that it's nearly too late. She can't hear me. There she is, shut in between partition walls, listening to other people who mean nothing to her cry. Maybe it's something to do with the biological bond, which wasn't there. Maybe he was a stranger to her body, a cuckoo's child after all.

That I am that woman is something I can't understand.

Initially the police thought he had run away, that he'd turn up soon enough. In those days I searched for him alone, hanging up notes, driving around town for hours. I stopped whenever I saw a boy who resembled him in any way, anyone who looked like him from the back, from a distance. After going on like this for a long time, I began to suspect people of having swallowed my Kito, having stolen his smile or his way of walking, hiding him inside their body. Only his voice – I never heard that. I knew I wouldn't succeed on my own, I was realistic enough to realize that. When I was looking for him at the market I'd think, 'What if he's on the square?' and when I got to the square I'd think, 'What if he's on his way to the market?' Of course I stuck posters up on lamp posts. But it would have taken dozens of us to have any chance of finding him, and probably he was already dead all that time.

Later, when people finally started to realize it was serious, they did want to help. Neighbours, acquaintances, people from school – they offered their assistance in droves, but their initial enthusiasm didn't last long. For them, he was a way of passing the time. It wasn't about Kito, but about picturing themselves as the hero who found him.

I also walked through the dunes alone, and that was even worse. I didn't know where to look, or what I was looking for exactly. I knew I didn't want to find anything. Not his body, so pale now there was nothing I could do to make it better. I couldn't give him dried apricots or prepare him a steak or peel him an apple for the vitamins – I wouldn't be able to do any of that, because he'd never open his mouth again. I didn't want to find his body – I knew that, if nothing else.

In the evenings I passed by the sports fields where floodlights shone down on games played by boys his age, their mothers waiting for them in the car.

Sometimes I stood there all evening, in one of those car parks, watching all those mothers open the doors of their estate cars to let their sons in. Watching the light in the car go on briefly while the boy looked for the right radio station, before the mother started the engine and drove off with him by her side, the two of them safe in their Faraday cage. I would stand there as the car-park gradually emptied and the lights and the sound of the engines faded. Then there would be the boys on bikes, weaving their way home in their hoodies, the clouds made by their breath, their elated voices in the dark.

Kito was never one for sport though.

If he did have friends over to play, which wasn't very often, they were always the shy, awkward type. Even when he was fourteen – kids with glasses and trousers that were slightly too short, jumpers that weren't quite the right kind. Or shirts buttoned right up to the collar. They never said hello, they always looked down. If I was at home I would take up something to drink and there he would be, sitting up straight next to one of those scrawny, round-shouldered creatures who never took their hands off the controller of the PlayStation. 'Where's the fun in that?' I would ask Kito when they'd left, and he'd say, 'We're playing life after life.' I didn't understand at first, but then he explained that the other boy was allowed to keep playing until his avatar died, only that never happened. That was Kito for you: he just kept waiting for his turn to come around. Afterwards, whenever I saw one of those boys, I felt an urge to slap him in the face, the self-centred little brat.

Kito hadn't run away, he hadn't committed suicide.

Someone who can sit there all afternoon waiting for his turn to have a go on a games console, and not just once but again and again, that's not the kind of boy who runs away. Not towards something, anyway, not because he wants something he can't get at home, as the police put it. When he was little he was such a beautiful child. When I went out walking with him everyone would look at us, at him. The time we fed the ducks and the sun sparkled on the water. The time when, afraid to swim at first, he did it anyway. The time he stroked a dog. The time he threw a stone into the water and he saw how it made circles, and he wondered whether you could change water into stone. When it puzzled him that the drops of water splashing up didn't turn into a solid, heavy stone, and he kept trying it again and again. The time I pointed out the blossoms in the treetops and he opened his eyes so wide.

I was overflowing in those days.

Happiness is just another word, an empty signifier. But waking up every morning I would feel how everything in my body was on the verge of opening up. I'd become so strong and sharp in the years before Kito arrived. I wasn't a hospitable place anymore, I was no longer used to letting things in. Ever so slowly, he was making me more unfriendly.

When the police finally started to take us seriously they asked us for a description. Could we give them photographs, as recent as possible, and tell them what kind of boy he was? Who were his friends, what were his hobbies, what did he like to do? But how can you reduce your child to a handful of words? Kito liked flying kites, bird-watching and vanilla ice cream and even though he was fourteen ('nearly fifteen'), he could still be scared of the dark and wake up screaming from a nightmare.

Years before he disappeared he'd already retreated into a world where I couldn't reach him. He had become evasive and shy. I'd be waiting for him in the afternoon with tea and biscuits and the question 'How was school today?' and I knew he was going to say, 'Good.'

'Did you do anything fun?'

'No.'

And then he'd go upstairs, his expression unreadable. If he wasn't sat behind his PlayStation he'd disappear into the dunes for hours on end, with a sketchbook under one arm. Mark told me not to worry so much. It was healthy for a boy his age. We should count ourselves lucky that he had a hobby.

Later I made an effort to come up with questions he couldn't answer with yes or no, but that's harder than you think. Kito always found a way of saying nothing. He withdrew into himself to the point where he was hardly touching our world anymore. I thought it was a phase he was going through, puberty, something we would look back on and laugh about one day with him and his girlfriend, drinking a glass of white wine.

It was important to believe that, because if it wasn't just puberty – not just the usual anxieties about spots and girls – he might be worrying about the fact that we weren't his real parents, biologically speaking. We'd been warned about kids going off the rails even before we set eyes on Kito, under the fluorescent classroom lights during the Thursday-evening adoption course, during the interviews and assessments, the endless

11

bureaucracy of being expectant adoptive parents. Two social workers were authorized to judge whether or not we were suitable for parenthood, just because they had functioning wombs and I didn't.

The lining of my womb killed Mark's sperm: my body destroyed what he gave me. It was painful to hear but it didn't surprise me. It made sense somehow, fitted in with the awkwardness, the hesitancy with which he reached out to touch me. We weren't physical creatures, or maybe we lacked the courage to be vulnerable, to lower our guard.

We met at a Christmas market, even though we're not the kind of people who like going to Christmas markets. If we do go to that kind of thing we do it ironically, or even cynically. We go to watch other people.

That is to say, I do.

Because Mark genuinely enjoys the experience. He likes Christmas songs about love and he likes gifts you can give each other, no matter what they look like. That evening he was manning a stand for Amnesty International, where you could sign a petition to free a prisoner, another thing I didn't believe in. I was in my thirties and working long hours, and afterwards I was tired and I was in no mood for company, let alone conversation. But this Christmas market was happening right outside the place I was living, and the sounds crowding in through the window made it impossible for me to concentrate.

I wandered between the stalls listlessly, avoiding children who had some kind of luminous toy on their tongues, moving through the crowd too quickly, like a swarm of fluorescent aliens. There was a greasy smell of churros and grilled sausage. Everything on sale was rubbishy and cheap. Even the cheery atmosphere was kitsch, kept afloat by middle-aged couples walking arm-in-arm and saying how nice it was, their voices just a little too loud. Those were the kinds of things I thought, and then I would curse myself because those people were actually enjoying themselves in spite of it all.

Nobody was standing in front of the Amnesty stall, which is why I walked up to it. Without much interest I looked at the photographs of people who'd been imprisoned unjustly for too long, while an over-eager volunteer forced their stories on me. It irritated me and I wasn't listening until he suddenly stopped and said, in a very different tone, 'You look so terribly sad.'

It's insulting when a stranger says something like that and I was about to walk away when he asked me to come for a drink. The fact that I didn't say no was down to his hope against hope, the naïve quality that would have annoyed me in anyone else, and the fact I'd spent the past few hours observing a crowd I could not feel part of. I hesitated, but then he was already next to me, putting his arm round my shoulder, and to my surprise I didn't mind. At one of the stalls he bought a pair of warm woolly socks for me and said, 'You don't even realize you're cold anymore.' He was right. For the rest of the winter I wore socks to bed.

His telling me that, something even my friends would never say to me, that was him all over. Even after years of working in development aid, Mark still thought everything would be all right in the end and that everyone was basically good-natured. Perhaps it was the only way he could carry on doing his job. He gave money to people at stations who said their wallets had been stolen. He would cheerfully roll down the window for someone about to rob his car. And he started a relationship with me, as if he'd found a half-withered pot plant on the street and taken it home with him.

Unlike me, he was very good with children.

We hadn't been together very long, but I was at the age where all my friends and colleagues were having babies, sending announcements that I stopped replying to after a while. To begin with I would still go on visits, bending over cots with other women and admiring noses, eyes and tiny fingers. Sometimes Mark would come along, and unlike many other men he seemed good at that kind of thing, making the children laugh, knowing how to hold them as well. Babies made me feel uncomfortable. I couldn't handle their vulnerability, the trusting way they stared at the world, the softness of their delicate skin. It wasn't even a question to him whether we wanted children or not, and when I protested it was in a half-hearted way and he didn't believe me. 'You're scared, that's what it is. I'd be scared too if I was a woman.'

We were sitting on the lawn, in front of the house we shared by then. He had his arm around me and I didn't want him to let me go. I'd changed since we got together, become more vulnerable. I was feeling things I hadn't felt for a long time and wasn't sure I wanted to feel, even though, in the same situation, I would always encourage my patients. 'You want to live, don't you?'

I'd say. 'You can't live, not fully, without experiencing fear.' They'd look at me for a long time, as if trying to read my face for signs that they could trust what I said, but they almost always believed me.

'Maybe it's my profession. As a psychiatrist you see all the messed-up children, twenty, thirty, forty years later – shuffling, crouched over, burnt out – and once upon a time they looked like that too, when they were in the cradle.'

'You're just saying that.'

'No, I mean it.'

But he threw me on my back and tickled me until I couldn't speak, and I was desperate to believe in his carefree attitude, in that wholesome, friendly world he saw before him so clearly.

Initially the thought of having a child made us younger and more frivolous. We giggled and lit candles and started thinking of names for the child to come. Every month we waited and hoped. Suddenly, my period was his business too and later on there was something shameful in having to tell him, month after month, that I had failed yet again. He'd laugh it off, but the laughter sounded forced. I'd never really thought about my body before, but now it became my enemy, letting me down again and again. What followed were appointments with the GP and gynaecologist, the cold paper under my buttocks, my legs spread wide for yet another latex-sheathed finger.

Mark said, 'I used to wet the bed, and every night I hoped and vowed that it wouldn't happen again. Is that what it feels like sometimes, when you get your period again?'

It wasn't too far off, but I didn't tell him that. 'You wet the bed?' I said, and turned my head away when he wanted to keep talking. Because it was more than just my body. Deep within me was something dark and resentful and black, which was too powerful for Mark's poor sperm. A child would never be able to survive it.

A hostile uterus is what the hospital called it.

My cervical mucus and his sperm were incompatible, they said, and then apologized for the unfortunate phrasing. But it had already etched itself into my brain: we weren't meant to be together.

'These days people assume they'll be able to control all aspects of their lives, but sometimes there's simply nothing we can do.'

The gynaecologist was young and smooth. Clearly nothing bad had ever happened to him. I wondered if he'd finished his specialist training or whether he'd just been let loose in this place – a place for people who need an entire laboratory to do what any idiot can do naturally: conceive a child.

'Thanks anyway,' said Mark, who was often shy in unfamiliar surroundings. 'Thanks for everything you've done.'

It sounded like he'd actually got something to show for it, which made me want to pinch him hard.

'It can be difficult to deal with,' the doctor said. 'I understand that. Don't hesitate to ask for help. Of course, you are yourself a ...'

This was not the place to get the help he was talking about, that was clear from the closed file on the desk, the cap screwed back on the pen. These were signals

I was familiar with, I used them myself, and for a moment I was embarrassed by Mark, who remained seated, hopeful, as if he hadn't grasped the elementary conventions of this interaction.

I stood up, thanked the doctor, and walked away without waiting for Mark. Outside the consulting room, Mark's hand sought mine, but I crossed my arms and looked away. Making our way through the hospital we said nothing, following the brightly coloured lines to the exit. When we stepped outside we were strangers to each other, awkward and overly polite.

How long was it, after that, before the idea of adoption came up? How long before one of us dared say it out loud? How strange to have forgotten – the moment when our imaginary child's skin changed colour, the evening or afternoon when we decided our child could be someone else's.

When Kito was older, in primary school, I'd wait for him at the gate when my schedule allowed it, listening to the other mothers. They all seemed to know each other very well, and they all seemed born for their maternal role. Standing among them made me feel like an impostor. I tried to join in with the conversation, but my voice sounded artificial even to myself. I told them how he jumped onto the bed in the mornings and put his arms around me, how soft he was and how open. How he reminded me of something I'd forgotten a long time ago, how innocent he smelled.

They listened, nodding politely, but what I said didn't strike the right note and I had nothing to say about the history they shared with their children, the birth and the genes they got from this or that parent. They looked at Kito and thought he was a cute little thing, with his dark skin and the curly hair they all wanted to touch. I listened to them cooing and wondered what they'd think about him later, what they'd say about him at the dinner table if one of their daughters went out with him.

Gradually, I started avoiding the school gates.

Whenever the school sent out an appeal to mothers to help out (with reading, group activities, school trips, playground duty, decorating the classroom or staying over during lunch), more often than not it was Mark who pitched in. He became something of a celebrity at the school, because it was rare for a father to get so involved. The other mothers crowded around him like a brood of hysterical hens around a rooster, and the few times I did show my face at the school I felt even more of an outsider. I was sure they talked about me and how I didn't deserve a man like that.

At first, Mark tried to encourage me to come, pretending not to notice when I scheduled my late appointments to coincide with concerts or plays, and trying to drag me along anyway, on the evening itself. 'It would mean a lot to him if you came to see him.'

When I saw Mark again after one of those evenings, when we were in bed, he would tell me what he'd seen. He often took pictures or videos, which we would watch together, my head on his shoulder. At those moments I'd always make up my mind to go next time, but when I complimented Kito on what I'd seen in the video the next morning, I could almost feel his discomfort as he thanked me. I would imagine him and Mark on the drive home, Kito keyed up and talkative to his father, who was less critical than I was.

The longer I stayed away, the harder it became to show my face at school. Little by little, a gulf had opened up that couldn't be bridged; school had become a domain where I didn't belong, and this didn't change when Kito went to secondary school (although I did do other things, like make him sandwiches and put little surprises in his lunchbox, take him out to buy a nice new leather bag for his books and wave goodbye in the mornings when he set off on his bike).

We had a babysitter in when I was at work. I would come home and see that girl with my son and sometimes it seemed like he was her child – the way she bent over him, the way he looked up at her with complete trust, not noticing I'd come in. I'd stop in the hallway, looking at him, and then turn around. Then I'd come in again, noisily this time, so he'd call out 'Mama' and jump up, away from that other woman. But at night I would dream of the stately women I'd seen in his country. I dreamed of his real mother taking him out of my arms, not roughly but very gently, as if I'd just been minding him for a while. She took him and lifted him to her breast to feed him and I looked at them, my empty hands outstretched and my barren body rigid.

It was only after Kito disappeared that I noticed my work wasn't a reason to get up in the mornings. In those days I wasn't even capable of making myself a cup of coffee. I would spill the water, forget the filter, heap the machine with spoonful after spoonful of coffee before realising it was too much, and once the machine was on I would walk away and forget about it, surprised yet again to find the cold liquid in the evening.

I staggered and stumbled through the world.

When I touched things I felt nothing. Only my eyes seemed to have improved, registering everything with a harsh precision, and for a long time that was all I was, a pair of eyes, observing everything but feeling nothing. Dissociation is what I called it in my past life – it was a phenomenon I often saw in my patients. The word derives from *dissociare*, to separate or, more literally, to remove from society. Sometimes it made me laugh, after he disappeared, to think how often I had explained that to others. What the hell did I know?

When he was gone I only opened my mouth to say one thing: it isn't true it isn't true it isn't true. As if such a thing could be negated, could be pushed back to wherever it came from with words, I kept saying it wasn't true. Like raising a dam, reinforcing it brick by brick as long as I kept repeating it, as long as I kept saying it loud enough.

In the mornings I tried to get dressed but just stood there, in front of my wardrobe, looking at my smart trousers, jackets and skirts, the absurdity of it all. Kito's disappearance had removed all coherence from my life, and the thought of putting on one of those skirts, taking the effort to put on one of those smart jackets, made me laugh, laugh so hard it would make me cry.

Or I would look at Mark, at his combed hair and smoothly shaved chin, his tie which was always perfectly straight, and I would see that under all that neatness, the smooth and straight surface, something had shifted and faded irrevocably. Then I'd want to stretch out my arms to him, but I wouldn't. I'd just sit there while he

20

sliced the cheese and feel how I was falling short once again, how he deserved better.

I couldn't eat in those days, couldn't feed my body – it would have felt completely unnatural. But the whole time, Mark never stopped cooking.

The less I ate, the more ingenious his meals became: soufflés and osso bucco left untouched on my plate. I thanked him for cooking; he tipped the food into the bin. It got on my nerves: his friendliness, how carefully he avoided getting angry, and how he treated me generally, as if I could break into a thousand pieces at any moment. Wanting to provoke a reaction made me unreasonable, reproaching him for things that didn't really bother me, slamming the door when I left. I hoped he'd shout at me, but he never did.

After Kito disappeared, Mark stopped taking his suit jacket off after work, waiting until he went to bed to hang it up on a hook. Lying in bed, looking at the dangling fabric, I'd think maybe that's where Mark's grief was, in that emptiness, the hollow space between the arms and collar, not in the body lying beside me. Though that's what I longed for: someone who grieved for Kito the same way I did, so we could be deranged together.

You can't 'conquer' this kind of grief, it never goes away.

But apparently you can make a deal to pretend to ignore it. That's possible: deciding you want to be happy again, or at least pretend you are, deciding to give it your best shot. You can tame your grief, apparently, or some people can. All Mark needed was a new patio with an awning.

I thought we'd stay indoors for the rest of our lives; the walls of our house had become a second skin to me. Just the thought of it – visiting friends and running into their children, coming across them by accident, having to see them change, grow older, while Kito was left behind, fading slowly. But one day Mark said, why don't we invite them round to ours, we could if this was a nice place to spend time in. I didn't understand what he was saying, how this could ever be a nice place again. That same afternoon I saw him lugging around a new set of wooden garden furniture.

'Maybe we can choose the cushions together,' he said. The hopeful look in his eyes made me furious. In the evening he stood in front of the window looking out at the patio and the two large wooden chairs standing there – just two.

'All we need now is a bit of shelter.'

I threw my food in the bin and went out.

When I came back the table had been cleared, apart from the candle which was still burning. Mark was in his chair by the window with his earphones on. His eyes were closed and he didn't notice me coming in. I said nothing, just looked at him, at his fragile back and his untidy hair. This would be the moment to touch him.

The next day I heard him talking on the phone – in those days we listened to everything the other person did – and a week later men came round to install the awning. I was furious because he hadn't warned me, had let them in while my grief hung round my face in limp strands, but he was happy as a sandboy. He hovered around them while they worked, and I heard him say, 'Some shelter, that's what we need', and they agreed with him, of course they did – he was paying. When you're paying you have the right to make a fool of yourself.

Meanwhile I spent hours sitting on a bench in the park, watching the leaves fluttering down from the trees. On nice days at the weekends families would pass by: a mum, dad and one or two kids. They stared at me but I avoided their gaze. As soon as they'd passed me the whispering would start: the kids' questioning voices, the parents' hushed response. I had become strange, a stranger now.

'We have to do something,' Mark would say sometimes, 'we can't just carry on like …'

His eyes wandered around the room, before fixing on the new garden furniture we'd never sat in together. Our marriage was a carcass, open at the spine.

Mark got up early in the mornings to go cycling, 40k every day before work. He shaved his legs to go faster. I watched as he tried again and again to grab hold of life and sometimes succeeded. I hated him for it.

If I had been Kito's birth mother, if I had carried him in my womb for nine months and only then released him, bringing him into the world with much pain and groaning and terrible contractions, if I had done that, I would have had something to set against Mark's shaved calves, I could have let out a primal scream. But we had picked Kito up like he was a postal package, and I had no more right to grieve than Mark did.

There were intermittent updates from the police – from Joyce and Walter, as Mark insisted on calling them, as if they were friends of ours – but there was rarely news.

There were no leads, nothing to explain why Kito had disappeared that evening after the class outing to the beach, or how he had ended up in the water.

'It's the sea,' I said, 'the beach, not a quay you can fall off by accident. How could something like that have happened?'

They didn't know. They interviewed the teacher who had taken the class out that day, Hannah she was called. His classmates said she and Kito had a special bond, that she spent extra time working with him. And yet I'd never even heard her name before.

Joyce raised one eyebrow very slightly when I said that, and I felt ashamed of knowing so little, now that it really mattered. But since Kito had started at secondary school, even Mark had lost track of the names of his classmates.

'Did he really never tell you about those drama lessons?' Joyce insisted. 'The extra lessons she gave him?'

'Extra lessons? For drama?'

She shrugged. That night I opened the door to his room for the first time in a long while. The bed was as he had left it, neatly made. He did that without needing to be asked, which was unusual for a boy his age. I should have been happy about it, but instead I wondered why, after all those years, he was still behaving like a guest and not like someone who was at home.

There was a time when I would open the door to Kito's bedroom quietly and stand there in the doorway, looking at his sleeping body. At his face, so open and vulnerable. Sometimes his eyelashes would flutter

24

and I'd be afraid I'd woken him; sometimes he'd toss and turn his head on the pillow like he was having a nightmare and was being pursued or threatened in his sleep. Then I'd make sure I tripped on something and made a lot of noise as I passed through the hall, back to the kitchen. There I'd get a mug ready and warm some milk, and it never took long for Kito to appear, just-abandoned sleep hanging round him like a warm, soft blanket. We said nothing but clasped our hands around the steaming mugs. And once he'd finished his milk he'd shuffle back to bed, while I sat there in the kitchen and watched him go. Sometimes I could see the man he would become; he'd been growing faster lately and the chubbiness that had characterized him for so long was starting to disappear.

At those moments, in the kitchen at night, we shared something that divided us during the day. It was the reason we were awake, while Mark slept unawares. He was unhappy, I knew that, and an outsider like me, and at night I felt a deep sense of pity for him, for all the years he had ahead of him, all the hopes he would harbour in vain, the attempts he would make to belong, to be part of something. But during the day, against my will, I felt my pity turn into irritation. I'd tell him to hurry up and stop moving his arms, his hips and his head in that way. He'd look at me shyly and I'd get even angrier because I had nothing better to offer him.

Later on, he started distancing himself, was no longer the child we'd picked up nearly fourteen years ago from a room where dozens of children stared impassively into space. Whenever I gave him a cuddle he would endure it politely, his eyes fixed on a future in which we would be no more than extras, a future I feared in a vague way. What a luxury, to be scared of something so vague and far away – but I didn't know that then.

When he went outside without his coat, when he came home late or had a sudden fever – sure, I worried about things like that, but always hoping, no, taking it for granted that my worrying would be enough to protect Kito. Because when it came down to it, we believed that was something we could take care of ourselves, that we were safe; that the ambulance wasn't on its way to us, and the police wouldn't appear at our door with their uneasy smiles, their serious faces. That was the deal: I spent hours thinking about what could happen, so it wouldn't actually happen in real life.

But fate was not the impartial referee I had taken him for, and didn't keep his side of the bargain (and yet: the promises you make, all the things you'd give up to get him back, the little wagers you still think you can make with a god you never believed in before, the cold heavens above).

The day before we left to pick Kito up, we posted cards to all our acquaintances to tell them about the child that was never supposed to have existed, but had come to us anyway. The cards had a blue satin bow on the front, and his name in ornamental letters on the inside, next to a photo, the only one without too much of a view of the depressing orphanage grounds. (The card was still in his photo album. He went through a phase of constantly asking about it – 'That's where I'm from, isn't it, that's where I'm really from; what was it like there?' 'It doesn't matter,' is what I'd say to him, 'you're here now, we love you.')

We invited everyone over when he'd just arrived, and everyone agreed how beautiful he was, such a lovely child, he seemed almost unreal. There were all the places we wanted to take him: the zoo, the beach, an amusement park. Though the adoption agency had warned us that the shock would be great enough as it was, that what he'd need most of all at the beginning was peace and quiet, that all the little everyday things were already enough for him to cope with. We talked about him so much we exhausted ourselves, and as we talked Kito became more real to us, more our own child.

And now there was no child. We were in a state which was the opposite to that of expectant parents, our future suddenly bereft of all our expectations. The only thing left was time, stretching out endlessly. How strange everything around us had become, so far away and so unimportant, and how slowly time passed, now that one minute could take hours, expanding and folding in on itself, and every day was a real threat we needed to survive. At night we would lie next to each other, incapable of touching, and if we did try once in a while we knew it was a mistake straight away. It wasn't right, because nothing was right now that Kito was no longer sleeping in the room next to ours, breathing peacefully. If he'd still been there we'd have been thinking about other things – about my patients or the situation in Nairobi or what colour the new sofa should be – but now he'd gone, he was all we could think about, day and night.

After the police had left that day, after what could have been hours for all I knew, after I'd screamed and screamed and screamed, after all that time, when it turned out really to have happened and wouldn't stop, after I'd tried to reach Mark and kept getting his voicemail but didn't leave a message because what was I supposed to say, after all that time I finally heard his key in the lock, the door opening, and before I saw him I suddenly felt how furious I was, how angry, because he'd been in an aeroplane, oblivious to my calls, and now dared to open the front door so calmly, so collectedly. I was furious because he'd had the luxury of thinking Kito could be out there, alive somewhere, for nearly a whole day longer. When he stretched out his arms, I started hitting him. I pounded his chest with my fists until he grabbed hold of my wrists, and the way his body felt told me he understood.

Later there was another visit from the police, Mark and me sitting next to each other on the sofa but not holding hands, not touching.

'Was he ...' Mark started, 'did anyone ...', but he couldn't bring himself to say the words. The officers looked down at their hands, as if they were visitors who had outstayed their welcome.

Just before I left Holland I saw a mother out shopping with – I presumed – her autistic son. She was looking at clothes, holding up blouses and jackets as if to ask his opinion, while he just rocked his upper body back and forth, a short blue strap connecting his wrist to hers. I have patients who are convinced that the well-being of the world depends on the way they brush their teeth or arrange their belongings, and as long as they

28

stay vigilant and pay attention at all times, the world order will be safe. It's our job to convince them that the small choices they make are unimportant, but since Kito disappeared I find myself thinking more and more often that they are right, and everything matters because you never know beforehand what your one crucial mistake will be.

The outing was nothing special, the school said, it was just Kito's class going to the beach to mark the end of the drama lessons.

Walter sounded bewildered: 'Shakespeare, something to do with shouting into the wind.'

I hadn't been aware of it, but then I'd been busy and maybe Kito had mentioned it in that offhand way he had, mumbling, not taking the trouble to open his mouth properly.

'Articulate,' I sometimes said to him, 'ar-tic-u-late,' and then he'd shrug and laugh a little. It seemed very important to me then, for him to learn to speak clearly and politely, to sit up straight and give his opinion in such a way that people would take him seriously. He was going to need it later on.

'What was your relationship with Kito like?' Joyce had asked. 'Were there any problems at home or school? Was he happy?'

But what does happiness mean to a teenager? How can you tell if a child that age is happy? If his sullen looks are just a sign of puberty or something else, something more serious? When a mother can't tell anymore it's up to the psychiatrist to make that distinction, but I'd failed in that capacity too.

'Did he ever talk about being bullied?'

'Was he being bullied? I mean, at *this* school?'

Kito had attended another secondary school before this one. Halfway through the school year he'd refused to go back. All he'd tell us is that his stomach hurt, and it was because of the school.

'But why?' I asked him. 'You know you can tell us anything, right?'

'I just have a stomach ache.'

Kito was vulnerable, soft. Maybe that's what I should have told the police when they asked me to describe him: look for a vulnerable boy. It wasn't what you'd expect, considering his start in life and the inevitable abyss inside him, the things he never had, the pain that must have crystallized in his skin. But Kito was chubby, his body and face had no hard lines to them, and even his eyes protruded a little, making him look like he was constantly surprised by the world. He usually mumbled when he spoke, and stuttered when he was nervous.

We could give him anything he liked, including an extra PlayStation so he wouldn't have to wait all afternoon for the other boy's avatar to finally give up the ghost. But that wasn't what he wanted, it would have ruined the game.

'What game?' I asked him. 'What do you do together?'

'You know, just play together.'

I knew why those other boys came here, and it wasn't for Kito's sake. They didn't even see him; they walked straight through to the PlayStation. Nonetheless, Kito had learned to speak their language, made up of numbers and abbreviations referring to prizes, weapons and enemies, incomprehensible to the uninitiated.

30

'What about trying sports?' I said, because I wanted to prepare him for the world outside and what would be expected of him out there.

'Wouldn't you like to give it a go, just to try it, I don't know' – I couldn't picture Kito playing football so I tried to think of a team sport that seemed a bit less improbable – 'handball maybe, or what is it you play at school, softball? You learn a lot from a team sport.'

In the end he agreed to try softball, a series of three trial lessons, probably to stop me harping on. He didn't want us to come along, he was very clear about that; but I still cancelled my appointments that first time, so I could follow him on the bike. The softball field was in a park and after I had parked my bike I stood among the trees, looking for Kito. He was far away from the other players, at the very back of the field. He didn't even pretend to be involved in the game, staring at the sky, the grass and his hands instead.

He never once looked at the ball.

At one point he turned away entirely from the other players, peering at the trees as if he knew I was standing there. I was too far away from the field for him to spot me, but when he looked in my direction I suppressed an urge to hide behind a tree. Eventually, he turned back, but not in time to go after a ball that had landed in the outfield. I could hear his teammates' cries. There was something very sad about the way he was standing there, slightly hunched over and a tad too chubby, a blissful smile on his face the whole time. I couldn't tell whether he was smiling because he thought things were going well or if it was out of sheer determination, an act of will. (We once took him to see a therapist, because he

31

still seemed emotionally detached. Later he told us the woman had said that if you just smile widely enough, you'll start feeling cheerful inside. Which explained why he'd been walking around with a deranged grin on his face.)

I couldn't stand watching any longer, nor could I pick him up after the lesson as I'd planned, with the excuse that I was just passing. I went home alone, cycling furiously so I wouldn't feel anything, and when he got home I didn't ask him how it went. He said he enjoyed it very much, a line he must have practised on the way back. He 'enjoyed it'; what kind of child says a thing like that?

'You don't have to keep going if you didn't like it,' I said. He looked surprised – giving up was not usually something I encouraged – but he insisted on going to the softball field for the two remaining lessons.

He threw up before the second lesson. He came home from the third with a black eye. He'd misjudged the speed of the ball, or that's what he told us.

'Well, that's what you have one of those gloves for, right?' Mark said, that evening.

'Would you like to practise with me, just us boys together?'

We were sitting in the garden. It was summer and still warm. A blackbird was singing somewhere. The garden was one of the reasons we'd bought this house years back. It was large, separated from the street by a wall. It had history, with deep-rooted plants, moss and flowers that seeded themselves – all I needed to do was prune. Now, in the middle of summer, we were surrounded

32

by an abundance of greenery, which was something I could appreciate these days. It was another thing Mark had taught me. Most of the time it made me happy to picture us, sitting there as a family, everything in its place, thinking how far I'd come. But now I couldn't rid myself of the image of Kito on his own in that field.

'You must tell us if something happened,' I said. 'If it wasn't just an accident.'

He said nothing, just pressed the ice bag more firmly against his eye while playing a computer game with his other hand. If he'd been a different kind of child the black eye might have been a badge of honour, something to brag about. I wanted to say something, do something to narrow the distance between us, but I didn't know how.

'We could start tomorrow,' Mark said. 'Just wait, you'll catch on in no time.'

'We just want things to go well for you,' I said. 'You understand that, don't you, that your happiness is the most important thing.'

The problem with adopting a child is that it introduced an element of choice we shouldn't have had. Did we want a boy or a girl? What age range? Would we consider a disabled child? And if so, what kind of disability and how severe? We had passed on our choices and here, nearly fourteen years later, was the result: a friendly, shy, vulnerable child who was always polite and never opened up to anyone.

'So, shall we give it a go?' Mark insisted. 'Just the two of us, practising together.'

He mimicked throwing a ball into the distance.

Kito looked down at his feet.

'Leave him alone.'

33

'I have a headache,' Kito said. 'I'm going inside.'

'Do you want an aspirin?' I asked, but he didn't answer.

He went into the house in that rather clumsy way of his, leaving Mark and me behind, sitting at the garden table. The hibiscus was in full bloom, weren't we lucky? I wanted to tell Mark what I'd seen on the softball field, but I didn't know how to start. We said nothing for a while, and then we started at the same time.

'He's unhappy,' I said.

'Maybe it's time,' Mark said, 'to ask him if he'd like to go back to see where he's from.'

'If he wanted that he'd tell us himself.'

'No, he wouldn't. He'd never come out and say it.'

'What do you mean by that?'

'Look, I know you love him,' Mark started.

'But?'

He took a deep breath but said nothing.

'Kito has no connection with that place – there's nothing there for him. It would only confuse him.'

That journey, that place. The heat.

How strange everything was in that country. How odd to think this was where he was from, and all of it – the chaos, the colours and all the noise – somehow part of him. The beggars everywhere you turned, holding up their hands, deformed or otherwise, standing in your way and staying there, holding out their hands again and again. The men who whistled at me on the street, even when I was with Mark and quite obviously his wife. So much life, growing everywhere and rotting away again just as quickly – twenty fish in a puddle of

34

murky water, a gecko in our room, butterflies the size of my hand.

During all those sessions in which we had to prove our suitability as adoptive parents – any idiot can put a child on this earth, but if you want to rescue someone else's you have to prove you're up to it – during all those evenings in that deserted classroom, surrounded by drawings and plasticine models made by other people's children, the little tables which were too small for us, during all that time I never fully understood how different things would be over there and what that meant. That became very clear the moment the plane landed, or actually before that, when we were waiting at the gate back in Holland, along with the tourists and the people from there, the women wearing elegant, towering headdresses and the men in simple clothes.

I didn't dare look them in the eye.

I was afraid they could tell just by looking at us that we were going to their country to come back with a child that didn't belong to us, even though we looked just like all the other tourists in our thin, overpriced clothes. Feeling their stoical eyes upon me, I looked away or smiled in an overly friendly, almost submissive way, which was just as bad.

After the plane had landed we made our way down the steps, the last off the plane, the heat lying in wait for us like a mean dog. The air shimmered above the tarmac, and there were some low green trees somewhere in the distance. Then the arrivals hall, which was shabby and overcrowded and very different to the sterile airports I was used to. It took more than an hour for all the luggage to arrive, while around me the women

35

sighed and fanned themselves. They were so stately, so voluptuously themselves. I'd never been so aware of the whiteness of my skin and how thin my lips were.

'I can't do this,' I said to Mark that evening. We were in one of those hotels you find all around the world, always more or less the same. 'I don't have what they have, I'm not like them.'

I was sitting on the bed, which was too soft for the emotions I was feeling. He was at the window, his back turned towards me. Panic was flapping around inside me like a bird frantically trying to escape.

'What if he needs something I can't give him, what if it's not enough?'

'Look around you,' Mark said. He pulled aside the curtain and opened the doors to the balcony, letting in light, stench and noise. It was so hot I couldn't stop sweating, but even the smell of my own sweat was different here.

'Come here. Look how poor they are. What does he need that they can give him and we can't? What do they have here that we don't have, or can't get?'

That afternoon we had visited the orphanage. We had seen him. The moment of recognition I had hoped for didn't happen, there was no immediate connection. At first I thought he hadn't even noticed we were there, because he kept staring ahead of him and running his finger along his blanket, again and again.

Later he laughed, when Mark tickled his chin. He laughed and kicked his little legs up in the air. Mark bent over him, tickling his side, and he laughed even harder and Mark laughed too, and I stood there looking at them.

We knew other adoptive parents with children from this orphanage. Each time a couple was united with their child they'd invite all the other parents round to look at the pictures and videos they'd taken. These were strange, uncomfortable evenings, not least because we were expected to admire the new child, who was often still rather skinny and shy, their skin ashen. Time after time, I had looked at the photos others had taken of Kito; I'd listened to what they told me about him, but his face seemed to change each time, and I hadn't even recognized him when we arrived. I looked on from a distance as Mark became a father and the baby a son. A young nurse walked up to them and clapped her hands approvingly, but I was unable to move closer, even when Mark called me. 'Look, just look at the little guy!'

I'd wrapped my arms around myself and I could feel the nurse staring at me, alarmed by my strange behaviour, so different to that of all the other white women she saw here. To reassure her, I picked up the camera and started filming. I filmed my husband tickling his son, greeting him, welcoming him; I filmed a man and a woman and a child; I filmed three strangers. They looked like they belonged together.

'It'll be all right,' Mark said now, putting his arm around me. 'It isn't easy, this kind of thing.'

We looked out at the traffic below. Non-stop car horns and people shouting, street vendors loudly hawking their goods. From one of the houses, I couldn't tell which, came the sound of a woman screaming furiously, a child crying. I felt a cold force inside me, something icy that I couldn't control. It was irrational, I didn't need Mark to tell me that, and he'd never understand anyway. No, he would laugh until I joined in. And then we would both laugh together, and he would say, 'You're so silly,' and I'd laugh even harder. We would go inside, hand in hand, and after that it would be as if what I had tried to say wasn't true, had never existed.

'It'll be all right,' Mark repeated and I didn't contradict him.

We went back to the orphanage the next day. While Mark was filming someone else's baby, the nurse, an older woman this time, touched my arm, pointing at Kito's cot.

'He no good,' she said, frowning. 'He killed his mum.'

I looked at her.

'He killed her,' she repeated. 'That's why.'

The director, a small, plump woman hidden behind a pile of paperwork, wasn't surprised when we told her. When the mother died in childbirth the child was often cast off. Who was there to look after it, after all? It was also seen as a bad sign, but that was just superstition of course. She gave us a big smile and showed us the palms of her hands.

'Of course,' I said, nodding meekly as she began to complain about all those outdated customs in a reassuring tone, as if grumbling about the weather. I was hardly listening, but I was glad I hadn't taken him away from another, better mother. As if reading my thoughts, the director reached out her small, plump hand and let it rest on my waist, the rough skin of her palm warm against my lower back.

Things did turn out all right, although it took us a while to get used to each other. The three of us had become a family. We belonged together. We told Kito, 'All we want is for you to be happy and feel you can be yourself. We will love you no matter what.' But one day I found him in front of the mirror with lipstick on and I asked myself, I wonder who that is, the real Kito, and I wonder if we want to get to know that person as much as we said we did. I wondered whether we were strong enough and whether he was strong enough for the world around him.

During the adoption course we had learned about children who had received so little love in the past that they became incapable of receiving it later in life, because even affection can turn into a threat. I had encountered cases like that at work too.

What we were prepared for was a child who would scream, a child who would kick us and beat his head against the wall when we wanted to comfort him. We were prepared for rage. And we were prepared to do anything to make him feel better, anything we could to save him.

But he never seemed to need saving.

In the beginning he would get upset about little things. The tap not being completely turned off, or someone ruffling his hair, or when he couldn't wear certain clothes. Then we would say it was because of that time before. All those things passed, sorted themselves out. But at the same time, the period that went before, all the things we didn't understand because we weren't there to experience them, seemed to loom larger and become more important.

We encouraged him to do what he wanted, the things he really liked, but it was as if we were speaking a foreign language. Nobody had prepared us for his politeness, his extreme willingness to please, how impossible it was to pin him down.

I expected some big change, but it never happened. I expected a joy that never came. I looked at him and he looked at his feet. When I put my arms around him I felt him flinch, a barely perceptible movement. He didn't need me, I felt. I told myself that this was as it should be, that I was seeing things clearly, unclouded by hormones.

All we knew about him we had learned since he had been with us, and there was always that time before he was our child, when he came into the world covered in another woman's blood. The months he had spent in a country I knew nothing about and didn't want to know about, the things that could have happened to him that I didn't want to think about, everything that tied him to that place and not to us, the genes I was afraid of. Everything, even the softness in his eyes, the shyness we didn't share and the craving, all those things made him vulnerable. And so I tried to protect him, explaining again and again what was considered normal and what wasn't, what kind of behaviour would make him a target. He listened to me dutifully, trying so hard it was painful to watch.

Yes, he was bullied.

But it shamed me to admit it when the police asked the question. It said something about us and what we were able to give him. Our child was rejected by others because there was something wrong with him, a smell of fear or a way of acting that had set him apart from the rest.

I didn't say any of this to Joyce, who didn't like me anyway, drinking her coffee with measured sips.

'And what do you know?' I asked. 'It's your job, isn't it, to find out the truth and get to the bottom of it? Isn't it your job to tell me why this happened?'

She advised me to get professional help.

I didn't want to go to a colleague or anyone with whom I might have shared even the vaguest of acquaintances. So I went to a private therapist, not because I thought it would help but because everyone else thought it would and kept asking in hushed and respectful tones whether I'd talked to anyone yet. No, I'd reply, no, I haven't. Then they would shrug and say, 'You should, you know. Although I understand that must be difficult, with your job.'

The practice was in a 1930s house. I rang the bell and a woman in her late fifties opened the door, a pair of reading glasses resting on her ample chest. Speaking softly, she invited me in. She lit some candles and only then did she ask me what was wrong. I said, 'My son is dead.'

She swallowed hard and there was a long silence, too long, before she asked her next question. 'How do you feel about that?'

She cocked her head to one side like a squirrel, her glasses reflecting the light. There was a box of tissues on the table. I looked at the box of tissues and wondered if I would ever cry again, if your tear ducts could dry up for ever, and I thought of salt lakes and endless plains. She asked me, 'What are you thinking now?' I pushed my chair back. It was a stupid question and when I looked

41

at the woman, her curly hair and her smile, when I looked at her face I wondered what was the worst thing she had experienced and why she thought she had a right to say anything about this. So I stood up and made to leave.

'Our time isn't up yet.'

I didn't answer, just blew out the candle in front of me and left the room. I was still wearing my coat. After that, when people asked me whether I'd talked to someone I could say yes. Yes, I'd say, and nothing more, and then they'd shut up.

Less than a fortnight later Joyce came round with a note. 'Is this Kito's handwriting?'

I looked at it for a long time. It was his handwriting all right. His boyish, clumsy letters, far too small, spelling out four words: *I can't go on.*

She didn't need to say what she'd come to tell us.

'Where did you get that?' I made sure my voice was even, that I sounded demanding instead of desperate. 'Why has it turned up now – where did it come from?'

'His teacher found it in her coat pocket. She hadn't worn the coat for a while and she'd forgotten he'd given it to her.'

'How could she forget a thing like that?'

'She said it didn't seem important at the time, it was a long time before he died. Kids that age can be melodramatic, and mostly it doesn't mean anything. In any case, when she found the note again she came straight to us.'

'Did you question her?'

'We have no reason to doubt her story.'

'No reason? Why would my son pass a note like that to a teacher he hardly knew. Why not to us?'

She was no longer looking me in the eye. Something had changed now she thought my son had committed suicide, because who knows what the reason could have been.

'We understand that this teacher was someone your son trusted.'

'I've never even heard her name before.'

'There's so much we don't know about our children. When I look at my own ...' She cleared her throat. 'The investigation may be assigned a different priority.'

'You mean a lower one.'

'I'm sorry.'

She waited, but nothing I could say would convince her now. I was the mother of a child that had killed himself, no wonder I was in denial.

Real-life police had little in common with the detectives I knew from TV. When they were around, I was astounded by their impotence, but now they stayed away I felt deserted. The case was more or less closed, no longer a crime in their eyes – at least, not one that could be prosecuted.

Suicides are often unexpected.

This is impossible to deny given my professional experience, having inevitably seen – from the sidelines – how relatives are left behind, looking for answers, reasons or anything that will help them live with that unendurable, inexplicable act. I'd seen how deeply disappointed the nurses were each time one of their charges made use of their weekend leave and newly

43

acquired freedom to take their own life. Although we, the psychiatrists, were responsible for deciding the right treatment, they were the ones who'd actually been around the patient day in, day out, comforting and calming them down when panic overwhelmed them in the darkest hours of the night. Contrary to popular belief, many suicides happen without warning. This doesn't mean people who announce what they're planning to do shouldn't be taken seriously though. From a distance, you can't tell whether someone's waving or drowning. Nobody knows what a cry for attention sounds like exactly and at what point it turns into something else.

I knew all these things. But Kito wouldn't have walked into the sea. He wouldn't have done away with himself as the expression goes (the obscenity of those words!). I looked for the teacher he'd trusted so much, who knew him better than we did according to the police, but she had gone. The school receptionist told me her contract had expired and they didn't give out teachers' home addresses. I waited a week before calling again. This time I passed myself off as a neighbour of her mother's – who I claimed had had a nasty fall that morning – and after some urging I got a telephone number, an address. But the number was disconnected and there was an estate agent's sign in the window of the house, the living room inside empty and deserted.

Later I was standing in the playground, his last class photo in my hand. His classmates were with him on that last day. I know what his face looked like when he jumped into the deep end for the first time: a mixture of fear and pride. How he laughed when he'd tied his own shoelaces for the first time. They were there on the day he died for the first time.

And so I went to the playground and spent hours staring at the kids, who were unashamedly alive and so sure of themselves. Some of them I knew because they had helped look for him, but they didn't see me now, or pretended not to.

I bought soft drinks for the boys in his class, who were hanging around outside the bike shed in a group. 'Were any of you friends with Kito?' I asked, even though I'd never seen any of them at home.

The boys stared at each other and then at me.

'Us?' This was from a tall, lanky boy, clearly the ringleader. 'We were great mates.'

The others laughed, briefly.

'And your name is?'

'Timothy.'

I invited the boy to come to our house.

'That's very kind of you.'

More laughter.

'I can give you a lift right now.'

He looked me in the eyes for the first time. I crossed my arms and didn't look away. For the first time, I wore my grief as a mark of dignity. Once he realized that as well he shrugged. 'All right then.'

He raised his arm to show his friends that he was going of his own free will, that it was a favour he was conferring on me, but the group remained silent as we marched out of the playground side by side.

I drove him to our house in silence. It was strange to have a boy sitting next to me in the car again, strange to feel that angular presence beside me. When we got there I opened the car door for him, waited for him to get out and escorted him to the living room. In the middle of the room he stopped and looked around. I saw him take it all in: the bookcases, the Persian rug, the map of the world with pins marking all the places Mark had visited. Only after I pointed to the easy chair did he sit down, on the very edge of the seat.

'What do you know about Kito?' I asked.

He said nothing, sipping the cappuccino I had made him, keeping the mug in front of his face for as long as he could.

'What was he like, in class? What kind of person was he there? What were you doing at the beach?'

'He was quiet.'

I looked at him. He couldn't keep his fingers from fidgeting, and he moved about awkwardly in the chair, which was too large for him. He was different here than in the play ground, no longer the tough kid I'd taken him for.

He'd taken his baseball cap off when he came in and was holding it in his hands, playing with it.

'My son is dead,' I said. 'Something must have happened that day.'

'I didn't have to come here.' He stared at his feet.

'Were you his friend?'

He grinned, sticking his chin out. 'Richard loves Richard; that is, I and I.'

When I failed to react, he explained, almost boastfully, '*Richard III*. That's what we were doing at school.'

'My son is dead.'

We were both silent. I stared at him until he looked up, then held his gaze for I don't know how long, minutes maybe, before he looked away again.

'Were you his friend?'

'Kito was, you know …' He waved his hand about, looking at me as if that would make me understand. 'Strange. He wore flowery shirts.'

His hair was combed back with gel; spots formed red patches on his pasty skin. 'You know,' he said, 'a poof.'

He spat the words out.

'A poof,' I repeated slowly. 'What happened that day?'

'There was something going on with that woman.'

'What woman?'

'The one from Drama. It was something – I don't know, it was strange the way she acted, she had these ideas.'

'What kind of ideas?'

But just then I heard Mark's key in the lock and I stood up when he came in. 'Oh, hello there,' he said, and coughed.

'This is one of Kito's classmates.'

'I'll be going then,' Timothy said, making for the door. 'Goodbye, and thanks for the coffee.'

'What was that about?' Mark asked later.

'I told you, a classmate. He wanted to say how sorry he was about what happened.'

It was only when I said it that I realized how much I wanted that to be true. How much I wished that one of his classmates, or even one of those round-shouldered little friends of his, just one kid his own age had grieved for Kito, and not for his PlayStation.

47

When I went back to the school after that, the boy avoided me, laughing at me from the raised platform in the middle of the playground.

'What kind of ideas, Timothy?' I shouted at him, but my voice faltered and broke, and then one day the school principal came up to me. He'd brought me a coffee and wanted to put his arm around me, take me inside, out of sight.

'It's terrible, of course it is, but you must learn to let it go.'

He put the emphasis on 'must', not on 'terrible', and so I pushed the coffee away and shook off his feeble arm. ('You must learn to let it go.' How often had I heard that? They asked me to pour my grief, raw and bleeding as it was, into a presentable form. Could the run-over animal be screened off – was what they were asking – couldn't something be done to muffle its cries?)

Later Mark said I should leave the boy alone, and I could tell by the careful way he said it that the school had been complaining about me.

'That boy doesn't know anything, he's just a kid himself. It's difficult for his classmates, too.'

'Oh really? Difficult in what way?'

'They miss him, they have to move on too, they have to forget. We're lucky the parents didn't file a complaint.'

But my goal was to make sure they didn't forget, that they wouldn't just slip back into their little lives and carry on as if nothing had ever happened. No doubt they'd already tidied his desk. And so I was there every day, clearly visible at the gate, and just when I thought nothing else would happen, a girl came up to me. I'd seen her before, kissing Timothy.

'You need to leave him alone,' she said, walking right up to me until she was uncomfortably close.

'What did Tim do to you? Piss off!'

I saw disgust in her heavily made-up eyes as she looked me up and down – my ravaged face and sloppy clothes – and just for a minute I felt ashamed.

'I'm Kito's mother. Did you know him, were you in his class? Were you friends maybe?'

'It was that bitch from drama, she's the one who turned him funny. She's the one you want, not us.'

She turned around once, blowing her gum into a bubble, then popping it. 'If you bother Tim one more time, I'll rip that ugly mug off your shoulders.'

That day, you could smell the tang of the sea very clearly in the air. I closed my eyes and took a deep breath. Like the salty air could ever seem healthy again.

II

THAT'S FOUR YEARS ago now. He would have turned eighteen this year.

For everyone else his death belongs to the past, an event used to measure the passing of time – my God, is it really that long ago already. But not for me. For me his death has grown larger ever since, expanding day by day.

They say shared grief is half the sorrow, but this kind of grief – if grief is even the right word – is not like a loaf of bread you can grab, cut into pieces and hand around. Since he died, words feel different somehow, heavy and unnatural.

Mark and I still talk, but it's an act, a pretence we keep up. When we need to cry, we lock ourselves in the toilet and pretend we can't hear each other through the door. We inhabit this house, which is too big for us now, like two strangers, politely asking each other to pass the butter, and how each other's day was.

We only do it to fill the silence.

We're no longer the same, no longer ourselves. His death has destroyed the people we used to be. And our house is no longer the place we made it; instead, it waits impatiently for us to disappear. The silence has grown around us; we now inhabit what is no longer there.

I was never very good with people, not without my profession to hide behind, but it was becoming

53

more and more difficult to talk to others. What was I supposed to say when they asked how we were? Our friends and acquaintances no longer knew what to say, weren't sure what to talk about, now the subject of kids was out of bounds. Unlike me, Mark bravely persisted in asking about swimming lessons, hobbies and exams, but that too made them uncomfortable and shy. They were constantly asking us to forgive them because they were carrying on with their lives and, unlike our child, theirs were growing up. Giving them a tired smile was easier than trying to show them even the smallest glimpse of the reality we now lived, in which all the children carried on living except our own. People don't like being around someone they keep having to apologize to. They sent cards, in the first few weeks and months; brought round casseroles, offered their support and sat in our living room until I asked them to leave. No doubt they talked about us with great compassion, but also with a sense of relief that it hadn't happened to them.

This is the year he would have become an adult.

Is it a plan I have, a decision I have taken – does it even deserve that name? It feels more like I'm looking for a reason, an excuse for the fact that I'm still alive, moving further away from him day by day. It's like I'm looking for something to fill up all that time.

Finding out where that woman went – Hannah, the teacher – isn't difficult. In the evenings I ring the doorbells of her former colleagues, who speak to me from the doorways of their brightly lit houses. They don't seem to have a great opinion of her. The English teacher, an older woman, even goes so far as to call her dangerous.

'How do you mean?' I ask.

'She didn't know what she was doing,' she said, sniffing bitterly. 'She gave them illusions. You always give them illusions, but some are more dangerous than others. Maybe she was too young.'

'Was it her fault?'

She just shakes her head, not prepared to say anything more.

The only one who lets me in is a friend of hers. She's called Maureen and she has a child on her arm. She also has dark circles under her eyes; she seems eager for company. 'The other teachers didn't really see the point of the subject she taught. That puts you in a vulnerable position. And Hannah is …'

She stops. She says how sorry she is, that she went to the funeral. She waits while I stare at her, because I can hardly remember anything about that day, that whole period.

'I haven't spoken to her in at least a year,' she says. 'That's just the way it goes.'

She strokes the child's head and I force myself to look away. 'The way she ran away from here, that wasn't good. You're a psychiatrist, you said?'

She wants to tell me more but the child starts crying and doesn't stop. I look around the small living room, the plastic toys lying everywhere. She looks at me and shrugs apologetically, picks up a pen and paper, and jots down Hannah's details from memory. 'She's in Bulgaria,' she says as she sees me out. 'A new life.'

For three days I walk around with that piece of paper. Hannah has a new life. Those are the words I keep repeating to myself. Kito is gone forever but Hannah has a new life. Kito is never coming back but Hannah ...

After the third day I start my email. I write about meeting Maureen and how she told me about the kind of life she, Hannah, was living over there. How it's the kind of thing I'd like to try myself. That I don't have anything specific in mind, but I'm not afraid of getting my hands dirty. A reply comes, sooner than I expected. She says I'm welcome to come and tells me what she expects from a volunteer – 'But make no mistake, it can be pretty tough.'

We fix the dates and I buy a ticket. I tell Mark roughly the same thing I wrote in the email: I need this to be able to move on, a change of scenery might do me good. It's painful to see how happy he looks, coming up with suggestions for places I could visit, things I could do. He gets me a travel guide, wrapped up as a gift. He insists on driving me to the airport. At departures we kiss awkwardly. We say goodbye, see you, I'll email you, and our words drop to the ground like stones. He keeps waving as I take my hand luggage through security, right up to the point when I turn the corner and can no longer see him, and maybe even after that. And yet putting some distance between us must be a relief to him too; we keep wounding ourselves on each other.

With plenty of time to spare, I pass through customs and wait while the official compares my face to the picture in my passport – a picture showing someone else, a smiling woman I no longer resemble. When he wishes me a good journey, I just stand there for a moment, surprised that he hasn't exposed me as an impostor. But it really is that simple – one action leading to another, narrowing down the options like a funnel. I need something to reduce the number of possibilities, a mechanism to carry out the motions for me for as long as I'm not able to.

It seems the summer holidays have started – yet another rhythm that has disappeared from our lives with Kito's death. All around are families en route to their destinations, the children shrieking excitedly, the mothers nervous. I don't hate them. I've put a lot of time and energy into trying not to hate other families and now, as I stare at the tall glass partition dividing us from the planes, all I feel is indifference. How strange it would be to look in at us from the other side of the glass. I picture a group of giants, at a great distance, and the way they would react if they spotted us: surprised and maybe even a little moved at first, they would soon become bored.

In the plane I close my eyes and try to move my body as far away as I can from the man next to me, whose sweaty hands grip the armrests. During take-off I watch the monitor, seeing the temperature drop and the little plane moving across the map in intermittent jumps. Outside, clouds form the polar landscape I thought was heaven as a little girl.

How could they have let me through security? Nobody gave me a second glance. I am a middle-aged woman after all, nothing special, and I'm not carrying any weapons. Neither do I bear any overly conspicuous marks of rage or desperation, or no more than usual for a woman my age, an infertile woman. I can't give life, but I can take it away.

Now the idea is out there it seems like the most obvious thing in the world. She must pay, whatever else happens, pay for what I will never get back, through a suffering equal to mine, however much that is. There's a balance that needs to be restored, there are things that can't be allowed to go unpunished. There's a fundamental truth to an eye for an eye and a tooth for a tooth that we no longer understand – until we are left eyeless and toothless ourselves.

When we land, the man next to me lets go of his armrests for a round of feeble applause. I'm the only one who doesn't immediately get out their phone, because there's no one to phone. I'm in no hurry to get up either. Only when the plane is almost empty do I take my bag from the overhead compartment and make my way past the stewardesses, avoiding their gaze. Bye, they say, goodbye.

It's boiling hot outside, the air shimmering above the asphalt. I'm the last to step onto the bus waiting to take us to the terminal, the last to pass through passport control. I've arranged for Hannah to come and pick me up, but after I've picked up my backpack there's no one waiting for me at arrivals.

I stand there for a quarter of an hour, waving away offers of transfers to Sofia.

The heat is making it impossible to think clearly, and for a while I just sit there in the shabby arrivals hall, watching my fellow passengers disperse. Finally, I pull out the crumpled scrap of paper with her number. As the phone rings I wait for the moment I will hear her voice for the first time, bracing myself for the shock.

The endless waiting. Calling his mobile, again and again and again. Not knowing if it was a bad sign to just get his voicemail, his polite voice. Calling and holding my breath when it rang, hoping against hope that he'd pick up and I'd hear his voice. Calling and dreading the moment the battery would run out, used up by my own desperate calls, fearing the silence that would follow. They only found the thing much later; before that the police saw it as a good sign that he'd taken his phone with him, a sign he was going somewhere or (they didn't say this out loud) running away from somewhere.

'This is Hannah.' Her tone is questioning, surprised even.

'Hannah, I'm at the airport in Sofia, we arranged to meet here.'

'Arranged to meet?' The questioning tone again.

'I'm going to be working with you as a volunteer. We arranged it by email; you were going to pick me up from the airport.'

Silence.

And then, 'I'd forgotten you were coming. Can you catch a train? Or wait, what time is it now? I can be there in two and a half hours.'

She's hung up before I can say anything.

While waiting I watch the people around me, the ones who want to leave this place. The women here wear staggeringly high heels, their hair is dyed either platinum blonde or too black, and their faces are pale despite the heat. The men are often smaller and more simply dressed. I don't know what Hannah looks like. I'm looking for someone with a hard face, a face like mine.

They say the eyes are the mirror of the soul. That isn't true. But I have learnt to always listen to my patients' voices, more than their words. I would have closed my eyes if I could, but that made them uncomfortable, as if my thoughts were more likely to wander if I had my eyes closed. Now, waiting for this woman, Hannah, I try to replay her voice in my mind, to hear who she is and how much distance I should keep. But the conversation was too short and it slips away from me. I know nothing.

Just under three hours later the first thing I notice is that she has a limp, dragging her left leg with each step. I stare, then look away, not knowing how to look her in the eye. It's obvious she isn't from around here; her nose is pierced and she wears her long hair in a braid.

'Hello,' she says, sticking out her hand. 'I'm Hannah.'

I smile at her.

It feels strange to smile at her, but then in primates smiling is a sign of attack. I pretend to be the kind of woman I'm not, stretching out my arms for an embrace she can't avoid. It's only when I hold her that I feel how skinny she is, how her shoulder blades stick out. She submits to it, waiting politely for me to let go.

'You lose track of time so quickly here – appointments, days of the week – you'll notice that yourself.'

I follow her through the small, drab arrivals hall, glad I don't have to say anything, not yet.

60

In my backpack I have some things for Hannah: a packet of chocolate sprinkles and a large piece of Dutch cheese, which will probably have melted by now. Despite these things, I am here to kill her. I shall get to know her and her truth, her story of what happened, what she did to my child, how she failed to protect him. And then, once I know what I'm doing, and her way of thinking, of laughing, what her face looks like when she thinks she's alone, when I know all these things, I will kill her. Kill – I repeat the word to myself to rid it of its strangeness.

There are other, better words.

To finish off, like a chore to be ticked off your list. To eliminate, like part of an equation. To dispatch, like you would a parcel. If I think long and hard enough I will find a word that attaches as little meaning to the deed as possible, a word that is almost sterile.

Outside, in front of the airport, an overweight father of five blond children frightens off a stray dog, which drags itself away slowly and stiffly. The youngest child shrieks encouragement while the man shakes his fist. Hannah shouts something I can't understand, and the man gives her the finger.

'I told him to leave the dog alone,' she explains. 'Bastard.'

She points to a light-blue Trabant, parked in a corner of the car park. 'That's it.'

The car looks like it should be in a museum.

'How far is it?' I ask.

She laughs and fiddles around with the key until she manages to unlock the car. 'These old Eastern Bloc cars are stronger than you might think. They're becoming a rarity here in Sofia, a collector's item, but in the countryside you see a lot of them, driving around or on the side of the road, eaten away by rust.'

The six-lane road leading to Sofia is busy, and the built-up areas on either side look disorganized. The car's jerky movements are very different to what I'm used to from cars back home. I see large billboards and run-down Soviet-era flats, washing hung out on tiny balconies. Hannah is having a hard time negotiating the heavy traffic. She's not assertive enough and other cars keep manoeuvring themselves in her way. She keeps her hands clasped stiffly around the steering wheel.

'It won't be like this the whole way, there'll be less traffic later.'

I just nod.

It feels strange sitting next to her in the car, dependent like a child. In the distance the traffic light turns green. Before three cars have had the chance to cross, it turns red again, to the sound of car horns.

'Why do you want to do voluntary work?' she asks. 'You could go to the beach or a hotel.'

'I want to get to know a different way of life.'

'It's not as romantic as you may have imagined,' she says. 'Sometimes it's so hot you feel sick. Then there are the mosquitos. You'll get bitten, you'll get a rash and be itching all over. You can still go back.'

'I don't want to go back,' I say, 'I just left.'

I wonder if she's regretting her offer to take in a volunteer, and I wonder what her life is like here. Is she dreading taking someone into her home, is she the one who's repelled by me, has Maureen warned her about me?

I look out the window and think of a book I once read about a woman who woke up one morning to find there was a glass partition separating her from the world. When I read it I was still young, still yearning for things. What made the greatest impression on me was the woman's cool detachment, how easy it was for her to kill her victims (despatching them, eliminating them, cold as ice). Cold: not being able to give Kito a blanket, make him a cup of warm milk, him lying there on his own in the water, in the cold and dark, already dead perhaps without me knowing it, with no one to tell him it would be all right, no one to take care of that.

We are now on a larger road, where EU signs leave no doubt as to who paid for the asphalt. We are overtaken by expensive cars and old wrecks, by rounded lorries that look like something from a children's book. Every now and then, everyone slows down suddenly, and when I look up I see ramshackle cabins, harbouring police presumably. There's never a car parked outside though, and I can't see any cameras: there's nothing they can do.

'Have you done voluntary work in a place like this before?' Hannah asks. 'Do you have any special skills? Do you know anything about, I don't know, gardening or woodwork?'

'No, but I'm a fast learner.'

'What do you do at home?'

'I'm a psychiatrist.'

She glances aside before fixing her eyes back on the road ahead.

'A psychiatrist, that must be interesting.'

My work used to give me a kind of satisfaction, though I didn't think much of my patients' helplessness, and I didn't see them often enough to establish a real connection. Their medication was a puzzle I usually found an adequate solution to in the end, a bit like doing maths. Some of them came to us after suffering a great loss, usually a divorce. Often they wanted us to be their parents, or a better version of them, someone who really understood them. It took time to make them realize that was a role we couldn't fulfil, and once they realized that it meant they were nearly cured.

I was good at my job, but I wasn't the understanding friend my patients liked to see in me. Their weakness often repulsed me. Their inability to keep their emotions in check and their capacity to abandon themselves to their grief struck me as a lack of character. I didn't understand how they could let themselves go like that.

I'd learned to hide it though, to keep listening, to make sympathetic noises at the right moments and ask the right questions. In the end, other people's problems were rather like heavy rain outside the window, which I observed from the other side of the glass. Sometimes they were grateful when they left, thanking me even more than the nursing staff, even though they were the ones who had done the dirty work. I shook their hands and felt like an impostor when they told me this place had turned them into a new person. They would always be afraid of the moment someone found out who they really were, deep down inside. Of course they could repaint their houses in shades called happiness and joy, but it wouldn't help them, wouldn't provide any security. And yet they still believed I had really helped them, had made them better.

Even beyond Sofia the countryside isn't as idyllic as I'd imagined; it looks messy, like a building site waiting to be filled in. We pass outstretched fields and later, further away from the city, low, round hills.

'You get a nicer view from the train,' Hannah says. 'It takes you through the mountains. You could do that on the way back, maybe. I don't know how much time you have.'

I ignore her implied question and she pauses, waiting to see if I will answer her after all. When nothing is forthcoming she clears her throat and asks, 'Do you like walking?'

Since losing him, I walk for hours. I walk at night, and keep walking until I'm exhausted and only then do I go home. Walking is the only effective anaesthetic I've found, more so than alcohol as it numbs my body and my mind at the same time. Once a police car slowed down beside me. Was I all right, they asked me, and should I be walking here alone at this time of night? I said nothing and gave them a hard stare. They repeated their question, but in the end the police officer shrugged and drove on.

I screamed at the car, but they didn't stop or do a U-turn. These were the people who'd failed to find Kito. I collapsed into a heap on the edge of the pavement and just sat there, while all around me it got lighter, very gradually. I wasn't aware I was crying, but apparently I was, because at some point a man sat down beside me.

65

He handed me a tissue, saying, 'I can't just let you cry here by yourself.'

It was good to feel another body next to mine. Before he left he helped me to my feet and asked me if I wanted him to call me a taxi, if I'd be all right.

'No,' I said. 'But thanks anyway.'

I walked away before he had a chance to go himself, and finally went home. Mark was downstairs in the kitchen holding a phone in his hand. He looked pale.

'Where have you been?' he said. 'I thought I'd lost you.'

He embraced my cold winter coat; I waited. He made a cup of warm milk and honey, but put it down on the table in front of me with a bang. For a long time after that I missed the man who sat down beside me. I missed him because he didn't expect me to love him.

I suddenly realize that Hannah is looking at me, and seems to be waiting for a reaction.

'Sorry, I didn't hear what you were saying,' and, because I'm not sure if she's expecting some kind of explanation, 'it was a difficult time.'

'Yes,' she says. 'Life can be difficult.'

After that she's silent again for a while. We are driving through small villages hidden among the hills and I look outside, relieved that I don't have to say anything. The houses here are low and it suddenly dawns on me that we'll probably be living in a house like that too, I'll be sharing a small space like that with her.

There are swallows on the electricity lines, and now and then a horse grazing on the dusty roadside. Through the open window I smell grass and dust and the stench of wood fires and melting plastic.

The people sitting in front of their houses watch us with interest. There are well-tended flowers in nearly all the front gardens, and large grapevines offer shelter from the sun. The plasterwork of the houses is painted in colourful shades of yellow, blue or pink. Despite this, all the villages look somehow run-down. Maybe it's the clothes people wear, or the dilapidated buildings from the communist era, or the newer, half-built flats, three or four floors high – depressing, unfinished frames already overrun by plants. Or maybe it's the trees, which look depleted, their leaves green but tough, not tender like those at home. With difficulty, Hannah avoids the potholes in the road and it takes a while before I realize that nearly all the people I've seen in all those villages are elderly.

We pass a lake and in the next village Hannah stops the car in front of a small house painted light blue.

'We're here.'

As soon as the motor stops, a dog starts barking wildly. I stretch my limbs and look around. The house looks like someone inside is happy or trying her best to be. There are yellow curtains in front of the windows and flowers creeping up the wall. A wooden gate leads to the garden.

'I'm just going to pop by the neigbour's, but why don't you go on ahead. The gate's open, I'll be there in a minute.'

She's gone before I get a chance to answer. I get my backpack from the back seat and hoist it onto my shoulder. I glance down the road. There's no one on the street and in the distance the hills merge into the sky, their edges hazy and indistinct. It's only now that I feel how tired I am.

I push open the rickety little gate and step into the garden; immediately, a large, dirty white dog bounds in my direction.

'There now, ' I say, 'there now,' before he can get to me, and then, when he shows no signs of slowing down, 'Down. Down, boy!'

For a moment I hope the animal just wants to play, but it curls its lips back and starts growling, a low sound from somewhere deep inside its body, then jumps up against me, its front paws against my shoulders. I stagger, already off balance because of the weight of the backpack, and fall backwards on the ground. At once, the dog is standing over me, its teeth just above my throat.

I'm scared to look up.

I don't know enough about dogs and the way they think. That's something a person can die of, not knowing about things they don't want to know about, like dogs and first aid, until it's too late. I don't know whether I should act like I'm dominant or submissive. I can't move and somewhere inside I'm surprised at my helplessness, and, in turn, at my own feeling of detached surprise. As if what's happening here doesn't really affect me, as if it isn't my throat the dog could sink its teeth into if I make one wrong move.

'Don't give them so much power,' I always used to say to Kito when he had another stomach ache and didn't want to go to school. 'Because that means you're doing it yourself, it's your own fault.'

He was so vulnerable, so sensitive; even an insect dying was too much for him. Some children are like that.

It was damaging, though, and made things difficult for him. We had to knock some of that sensitivity out of him because the world is an unfriendly place and, as good parents, we had a duty to prepare him for it. We wouldn't be able to protect him forever, shielding his eyes when bad things happened. But maybe this was the way he felt sometimes, the way I feel now, like a beetle pushed over onto its back and unable to get up. What was it he *couldn't go on with*?

The dog's the size of a German Shepherd and its low growling sounds threatening. But I still say, 'There now, doggy, nice doggy,' even though I am barely able to make a sound. 'All right, there now.' It's a ridiculous thing to say to a dog who could grab me by the throat at any minute.

Since they found Kito it was like my body was intent on taking risks, stepping into a busy road without looking, crossing just in front of a car. I fell and bumped into things and my shins were black and blue. My body no longer knew where it was. Back home, I avoided walking along the sea or tall apartment blocks, afraid of the pull the depths exerted on my body, afraid of my own desire to end it. Now that same body is just lying here, cowardly and deadly still, the dog's drool dripping on my face and its animal stench filling my nostrils.

'Get off, for Christ's sake!'

Hannah pulls the dog away with a jerk. 'Down, now!'

She drags the animal, now emitting a high, keening sound, to the other side of the garden by the scruff of its neck. 'She's scared of new people, she doesn't know what to expect. The trick is not to show her you're insecure, that's what sets her off.'

Don't give them so much power, I say to myself. As I told Kito so often, *You should never let them scare you*. He would look at me and nod meekly , just to shut me up. How do you do that, keep yourself from being scared? How do you reach that state – like it's something you can control. Only someone who didn't know what fear was could believe that would work. And yet it was my task to make him believe it, that fear was a matter of choice too.

'Do volunteers always get this kind of reception?'

'She shouldn't be off the leash.'

It's not an apology. I follow Hannah through the garden and across the veranda to the house. The dog growls at me from her corner of the garden, her lips still drawn back, and I'm relieved to be able to close the door behind me. I wonder whether the animal has sensed the reason I'm here, the way dogs do in films, and wants to protect its owner. And, if that is the case, at what cost? It's a factor to bear in mind, as is the deserted street, and no sign of police either. All factors that could result in complete success or utter failure.

'Tea?'

It's cooler inside. The room is small and practical. The wooden floorboards are painted blue and the doors dark red. There's a small stone sink in one corner, and a table near the window. Facing them is a wood stove with an old teapot on it. A string of fabric birds next to the window is the sole decoration I can see. The glass in the window is bumpy and uneven.

It's said that glass always continues to flow, and sometimes I think of that, telling myself that glass always sinks down to the bottom eventually, even though nobody knows when it will happen. Not long before Kito disappeared, I had a patient, a girl in her teens, who used broken glass to cut her thighs, just to feel something. She was the patient I talked to about dissociation, and although she did listen, I remember her picking at the long sleeves of her jumper while I talked. She was not beautiful or tragic, the way those girls always are in films. She was overweight, she had bad skin and she was deeply unhappy, and that was all there was to it.

Nothing I said seemed to sink in, but that could also have been down to the antipsychotic medication she was taking, which would make her even heavier and an easier target for the people around her, her classmates and father. It did mean she wouldn't notice it as much, would feel even less than before. I was no match for the desolation that hung over her, but I did try, talking until I couldn't take myself seriously anymore.

Now I'm here I no longer know what I'm doing, why I've come here.

'I have linden tea – that all right by you?'

'Great.'

She puts two mugs on the table and folds her hands around the teapot when she sits down, facing me. 'This kind of thing, making tea out of linden flowers, using dried mulberries in baking, it's still all new to me too. Back home we've forgotten about everything really useful – you wouldn't last one winter here on your own.

'Everything is so much more real here,' she continues. 'When I'd just arrived, everyone brought me cucumbers. One by one they came round, all the women. They always have cucumbers to spare, you can't eat them fast

71

enough and there's a limit to the amount you can pickle, that's true. But I appreciated the gesture, their taking the trouble.'

I take the chocolate sprinkles and the piece of cheese out of my backpack. She stares at them.

'I thought you might like something from home.'

'That's nice of you.'

Pushing back her chair, she stands up abruptly and takes the things over to a store cupboard. She places the cheese in a tin and puts the packet of sprinkles away. 'So the mice and rats don't get at it – you have to protect everything you've got here.'

She seems relieved, though, as she puts the lid on, happy to stow away the tin in her cupboard, next to the sprinkles, out of sight.

'So, what about you?' she asks. 'What are you looking for here?'

'What am I looking for? Should I be looking for something?'

'Everyone here is looking for something. That's what someone told me when I'd just got here and I didn't believe her, but she was right. You might not know it yet, but it'll come to you.'

I concentrate on smiling, clenching my jaw, using force if necessary to stop myself from saying what I'm looking for. My son's lost body, his smell which was no longer quite that of a child's, the uncomplicated way things used to be, when I was sure I knew him, had always known him. What I'm looking for is truth, a truth big enough to fill my body. An act of revenge that will satisfy the yearning I feel for my child. Naturally I don't say any of this; I blow on my tea and smile.

'That dog is so insecure,' Hannah says, 'she needs to be able to trust that she's the weakest and will be treated that way. You have to command her, grab her by the scruff of the neck, that's the kind of thing she understands. You mustn't try to be nice to her, it confuses her.'

One day, the girl who cut herself with broken glass went to the local train station and casually threw herself away. We thought we were making progress, that we'd made a connection. She sat across from us smiling, talking about the horse she took care of at the stables. After she died, her mother showed us her diary: huge, angry letters, filling the whole page, furiously etched into the paper.

'Being mean to animals is not a habit of mine, but if you're not careful they dump all the sad cases on your doorstep. The Bulgarians all know how sentimental us foreigners are.'

There's a long silence and I can't think of anything to say. She seems relieved when she can get up to show me the garden and the room where I'll be sleeping. The outside toilet is no more than a hole in the ground.

'It's all very basic,' she says, 'but you'll get used to it. And if you don't, you're not suited to being here.'

Adjoining the house is an extensive plot of land, largely overgrown with what looks like a type of grass.

'Weeds,' Hannah says, pointing at it, 'tough, though. It's the only thing still growing here in July and August.'

I follow her up the hill and have to suppress the urge to keep looking at her bad leg, her lopsided gait. It doesn't seem to bother her, though; she walks quickly, telling me about her plans along the way, pointing out the fire pit,

73

the compost heap and the vegetable garden, the chickens in their coop. I see corn, courgettes and tomatoes and a few gigantic pumpkins growing on one patch.

'So, this is it,' she says, as we stand next to each other on the top of the hill. She makes a sweeping gesture, taking in the house and the field. 'This is the whole world.'

I see the edge of the forest with fields in front, some of them full of sunflowers, and, closer still, houses with roofs of narrow, yellowish tiles. Somewhere in the distance there's the sound of tinkling bells.

'The goats,' Hannah says, proudly, as if the animals belong to her. I look at the house, the field, the tomato plants and their bright-red fruit. This garden is growing on my son's body. All her happiness springing from all the things he can no longer do, feeding off his death.

'I'm very tired,' I say. 'Do you mind if I lie down for a while?'

'Course not,' she says, with an underlying note of disappointment, 'you have a good rest.'

She turns around and starts plucking at a plant, randomly it seems.

All afternoon I lie on the mattress she pointed out to me, while the temperature outside continues to rise. The fact that she's human, a person who laughs and talks and does ordinary things, is something I had thought of but never actually felt before. She's also younger than I'd imagined. I wonder if I would have liked her if I'd met her in the street, not knowing what she'd done, or if she'd been one of my patients.

The room is square, with a small window, a low ceiling and thick, white walls. Thick enough to withstand the snow in winter, I imagine, keeping the cold out and the people inside together. A scream wouldn't be heard easily through these walls. And who would listen to it, what do the Bulgarians care about the life of a westerner, our soft, pale bodies. What is she doing here, what is it she's found here, why has she come to this place where there's nothing but barren earth and withered grass? It's a landscape that's finished and done with, awaiting destruction by a new age. She came here to escape, that's what matters. In fleeing from a crime, the criminal proves their guilt.

I spread out my things, take my clothes out of my bag and neatly refold them. Then I line up the piles of clothes until the space around the bed is covered by my things. I need to make this space my own at least, occupying it, conquering it. While I am thinking these thoughts I fall asleep. I dream of having killed someone, my hands dripping with blood, too much to hide. When I wake up it's no longer bright outside and for a moment I don't know where I am, what the noise is that has just woken me, who's knocking on the wooden door. 'You awake yet?'

I keep quiet, pretending I'm asleep, not moving as she peers in through the pane. 'Are you still asleep? There's food if you're hungry.'

How can I face her across a table, eat with her? It's only much later in the evening that I force myself to get up and go to her, yawning demonstratively.

'You've been asleep for ages. Here, you need to eat.'

The salad consists of roughly cut chunks of tomato, cucumber, feta cheese and black olives. To my surprise, I feel hungry. 'Do you want some *rakia* with that?'

I decline and she pours a glass for herself, throwing it back in one go. She refills the glass and watches me eat, her arms crossed.

We don't talk much to begin with. She tells me what needs doing: weeding, fence-building, whitewashing – smoke from the fire leaves a greasy black residue on the walls – picking up milk and eggs from the neighbours. The tasks she gives me are simple but tiring. My ignorance about plants doesn't help; even after Hannah's explanation I still don't see the difference between the ones I should be weeding out and the ones I should leave alone. Sometimes I feel her staring at me while I work, but I never look up. I work until my back and arms hurt, until my legs feel weak and I can hardly stand.

It's a relief to be able to work, to exhaust myself. Moving around makes the temperature a little more bearable; the moment I stop, the heat presses in on me. I lick a drop of sweat from my face, and the taste of salt surprises me.

I haven't cried in such a long time.

In the evenings I study her bookshelves in an attempt to find out who she is. Shakespeare's collected works, airport thrillers and *Teach Yourself Bulgarian, the Easy Way*. We read together, in silence. I stare at the Bulgarian alphabet, incomprehensible to me. Now and then someone calls and Hannah speaks to them in English. She cooks, making salads and pumpkin pies, baking her own bread. I watch her hands cutting the pumpkin, her strong hands slapping the dough. She's very young, she could be my daughter.

I eat the food she puts in front of me.

It's a strange feeling, being fed. As if being here with her is making me grow smaller, turning me into a child. In the mornings she tells me where to go for milk and cabbage, hands me some *leva* to pay with, and off I go. In the evening she lights the stove in the room I sleep in, saying, 'If you're planning to stay on, you'll have to get the hang of it yourself.'

It's a relief that the toilet's outside and we don't have to share those intimacies. I'm happy to have an excuse to go out when I need to. We haven't discussed how long I'm going to stay. Each morning is a new day, another series of chores, lunch, more work, and then the evening meal and silence.

I watch her, and in the evenings I try to describe what I've seen. I make notes of things that strike me, as I would with a patient, trying to find words for things I can't interpret.

We don't say much and avoid looking each other in the eye. The silence between us is uncomfortable. It's the kind of silence that develops between two people who usually rely on others to start a conversation and keep it going. I lost the knack of talking about nothing after Kito disappeared; maybe she never had it to begin with. She seems the type to resist empty chit-chat, always yearning for deeper meanings. Amid the silences there are short bursts of energy, when she grabs me by the arm to show me something outside, a plant that has come up against the odds, a gigantic grasshopper or spider – all the insects here are big, they must thrive on the heat.

'Can you imagine how happy I am here?' she asks me when she points these things out.

But when she talks about her life here she always sounds a little too cheerful, artificial, like she's prepared a story. I imagine she spends a lot of time polishing her experiences to present them to someone, another person, who may not even exist.

Now and then other foreigners come round to eat, people in their twenties, the guys in checked shirts, the women in dresses that look too delicate and graceful for the surroundings. Hannah introduces me, saying, 'This is my volunteer.' My working for her has become my defining feature, the only one that matters.

Her friends shake my hand but don't look me in the eye, their gaze wandering off even as they stand in front of me, to some feature of Hannah's house or garden, new or recently repaired or collapsed since the last time they saw each other.

Sometimes Hannah says, 'That's her work, she did that.' And to my own surprise, I feel proud. But again, there's little or no response from her friends. They say 'good job', but their eyes have already moved on. Unlike them, I'm only here for a short time, I won't be staying, and that's why they aren't really interested, don't make an effort to get to know me. All they talk about anyway is houses and plans and organising things.

I have nothing to say on those subjects, so instead I observe from a distance, watching Hannah with these people she calls her friends. She laughs with them and gives them food, but all the time she clenches her fists in the sleeves of her jumper. I watch the young men, their skinny torsos and muscular arms. Kito wasn't that much younger, could have been one of them if he'd been around a few more years. Even while thinking that, I know it isn't true. Still I picture him standing there between those lads, a skinnier and tougher version of the boy I knew, his arms round a girl's shoulders, cool.

At first, Hannah gives me my tasks and then goes off to do something else, usually far away, at the other end of the field, or inside when I'm outside and vice versa. She's a small form in the distance, a frozen figure. But her body still harbours the memories of a different time, a carefree, cheerful side she shares with the Bulgarian neighbours but not with me. Sometimes she roars with laughter when the old man from a few doors down pulls faces and makes jokes I can't begin to understand. Once I saw her dancing with the woman from across the road, her body supple, perfect despite her disability.

The dog continues to growl at me from the corner of the garden.

What brings us closer is the rhythm of our hands, pulling the bindweed out of the plumtrees, throwing them on a pile and setting them alight, the flames flaring up metres high. For the first time we are working together and that changes something, even though a certain distance remains. I try to forget why I'm here, to forget she's the only one who knows what happened and that the kids said it was her fault.

Each time I remember I have to leave the room.

Outside I cram my fist into my mouth to stop myself from screaming and pinch myself until I can think clearly again. I've told her I get bouts of hyperventilation and that no, I don't need a plastic bag to breathe into, but thanks anyway. Sometimes I can feel her eyes on me. I know that look, full of pity, I've seen it far too often since Kito died. Undoubtedly she'd like to give me advice on how nutrition, meditation or restful colours could change my life for the better. I hate advice, because nothing is that easy. Hannah has restrained herself up till now, and when I catch her looking at me like that I have to control myself, concentrating on a fixed point in the distance, clenching my fists, counting to a hundred.

But then I was never used to showing my feelings.

I've sent Mark a message saying it's doing me good being here, and the peace and quiet is just what I need. Telling him not to call me. I ignored his request for my contact details. There's this world here, this house, and then there's that world over there, a house that seems increasingly unreal.

I always go to bed first, pushing the cat off my lap as I get up, wishing Hannah goodnight from the doorway, and closing the door carefully behind me. I squat down in a corner of the field to pee, ignoring the barking of the dogs here and further away. As I walk back to the house I often look in at the window and she's always sitting in exactly the same position, her face hidden behind her hair. She never seems to read when I've left the room, she just stares into space as if the book was a pretext.

On Wednesdays we go to the market that descends on the village in the morning. She looks at pliers, wire and padlocks, and exchanges a few words with the market trader, who praises his goods. She then moves on to the woman selling second-hand clothes and rummages through the bins, holding up jumpers and T-shirts to inspect them. She looks like she genuinely hopes to find something nice among all that trash. I watch her, fascinated; it makes her seem vulnerable suddenly.

Later that afternoon she wears a shirt she bought.

'Nice, isn't it?' she asks and I don't know what to say. She laughs.

She often laughs at moments I don't understand, or about things I can't see and she doesn't point out the joke. She's not fond of sharing her laughter with others.

She wasn't always like this, that is becoming increasingly clear. I see it in the way she held up that shirt, for example: it wasn't vanity, but a memory of it. I watch her, making observations, and at night in bed I write down what I think I've seen. For the time being I know nothing, my notes are full of question marks and maybes. I think of archaeologists uncovering a city layer by layer, using a brush to remove the dust from the smallest objects, laying bare shapes and contours. I have to set to work like that, it's the only way. As long as I can see her as a subject, an object of study, a project, as long as I can immerse myself in her life like she's just another patient, I'll be able to keep it up. If she's a language, I need to learn her; if she's a landscape, I need to lose myself in her until she gives up her secrets and tells me what I need to know of her own accord. Now it's getting colder she's started wearing a black turtleneck in the evenings. It's too big for her and she pulls her knees up inside it, disappearing into the jumper like a child.

There's the irregular sound of her footsteps.

81

In the mornings the cows pass by with bells round their necks. The cries of the woman herding them, a tiny figure with a long staff, is the sign to get out from under the warm covers, splash my face with the ice-cold water from the spring and go inside, where Hannah's waiting for me.

In the afternoon a car passes through the village, a loud speaker proclaiming something incomprehensible. 'Gypsies,' Hannah says, 'they buy scrap iron.'

There's something reassuring about not under-standing anything, not even the way they waggle their head here to say yes, *da*, not even the alphabet. Let alone the things the *babas* say to me, the wiry old women, their grey hair in braids under a headscarf, who stop me in the street and take the trouble to speak to me in what are no doubt simple sentences. Laying a bony hand on my arm, their face intent on mine, they keep repeating the same words, as if I'm bound to understand if they just talk loudly enough. I turn my palms up, raise my eyebrows high and widen my eyes in an apologetic *ne razbiram*, I don't understand, and ultimately that's enough for them. They laugh and snort, and then they carry on with their work. There's plenty to do: they lug around buckets, work their land, and in between they raise the few children who are still here.

If I stay here long enough I will learn the language eventually, or that's what I imagine. If I stay here long enough and keep listening, the words will seep into my brain and slowly forge a channel. Eventually I will understand what the old women are saying and maybe lose my own language at the same time.

Sometimes in the evenings they beckon me to come and join them in front of the house. I do, even though

I am too big for the rickety wooden benches and feel embarrassed while the woman next to me talks to me, patting my knee gently now and then. One time Hannah was passing by and saw us sitting there. She joined us, translating some of what the *baba* said: that she's lonely, her family has left and the village is so empty, and the neighbours left long ago. I'm reminded of my grandmother, her old hand on the tablecloth and the way she cried for her dead son. But these women have something that doesn't run in our family. It's something to do with their bodies and the way they are planted more firmly on the ground. The *baba* embraces me when we leave and I am strangely moved, as if she's bestowing a blessing on me.

In the evenings, the cows make their way home slowly and the goats much more quickly, flocking around the spring. Their little bells jingle as they jostle and push each other aside, before taking off again with a jump. The woman who herds the animals shouts at them, but laughs often and loudly too, and at night she throws back the beer she is offered by the men who sit outside with *rakia* and sausage under the light of bare bulbs.

And so the days pass.

When Hannah finally starts to talk, really talk, it starts with a question.

'Why are you here?' she asks.

'What do you mean,' I could have answered, or 'You know, to help you out.'

But what I say instead, I don't know why, is, 'I have … I lost, a child.'

She doesn't say 'sorry' or 'how terrible' like most people, nor does she look away as I stumble over words that have nothing to do with Kito having gone forever.

She just nods, as if it doesn't surprise her. She looks at her hands when I start to hyperventilate, because I've never said those words out loud before. Back home people knew; people thought they knew. For them, the loss of my child was a disfigurement, something they looked away from out of politeness and embarrassment and tried to contain using clichés. But she says nothing, which is why I repeat it, 'I have lost him. I lost him.'

Because suddenly that seems the best way to describe it, that I lost him, maybe long before I even noticed.

We say nothing more that afternoon, but work instead. She sends me to the stream to fetch clay, and I let the cold water numb my hands as I scrape the fine, blue clay from the bed. I throw it in a sack and once it's full I drag it across the field and lift it into a wheelbarrow and then push that wheelbarrow along the road to the house. I do it once and then again and again, and the sack is so heavy that I can hardly put one step in front of the other. I don't have a child, I lost him. While I walk back to the house the clay on my hands dries, cracking and turning grey. If I fell now I would break.

'Tell me about him,' she says later, when it's evening. She fired up the shower for me so I could wash, and I've scraped every last bit of clay off my skin.

'Tell me about him.' And, when I remain silent, 'Tell me who he was.'

I hesitate.

84

But I long to talk about him. It's something I haven't done for so long, haven't been able to do because there was no one who would listen. 'One thing that disappears suddenly, something that has always been there but then suddenly isn't and you don't even know how long it's been gone, is that sweet, milky smell young children have, uninhibited somehow. Not even their sweat smells bad and then, all of a sudden, it's gone and they smell as hard and angular as everyone else. That's exactly the age he was, the age when that changes.

'Because people usually ask me that, how old he was exactly, as if it'll help them classify his death in some way, as if fourteen is different from thirteen or fifteen.

'Seeing him change like that, it was one of those times when you're not just happy but aware of it too, and you know it will pass and it almost hurts.

'Do you know what surprises me now?' I asked. 'That we get up every morning and go to work or school, trusting nothing bad will happen. Trusting the sirens we hear aren't meant for us, or for someone we care about, that they'll remain at a distance, far enough away to be interesting. Trusting we will come back, as ourselves, as the same person we were when we closed the door behind us, without bothering to say goodbye. Trusting nothing will happen to destroy us, demolish us, leaving us an empty shell. That we come back and eat our dinner, waste our evening on things that don't really interest us, go to sleep and then do the same thing over again the next day, that we're able to say "see you later" casually and trust that rhythm to carry on.'

She doesn't answer, and we spend the rest of the evening in silence. But there's an openness in her face that is new, and maybe something in her voice when she says goodnight later, or possibly it's the silence, which doesn't feel uncomfortable for once.

That night in bed I can't sleep. Why give her my memories, all I have left, when it's crucial they stay as they are, untouched and vivid and real. Because things like that, memories, thoughts, wear away when you share them. They fade, becoming sullied and stained: one ill-judged comment can distort everything. The way the police had created a new version of Kito every time they talked to us, until the whole room was full of cardboard cut-outs of our son, with Mark and me on either side.

Once upon a time, a small, soft boy was the centre of our universe. We talked to him, we fed him food and words and saw him grow plumper, healthier. We smiled at him and he smiled back, we stroked his curly hair and he beamed at us. And in the evenings when he was sleeping and we lay next to each other in bed, with no reason to touch each other anymore, we would talk about the person he would become. He would probably want to play an instrument later on, he was so sensitive that he might become a psychologist, or perhaps he would like drawing, and did you notice how quickly he figured out how that worked, maybe he'd do something technical instead? And so we constructed a son, a future for ourselves and for him as well. We bought him a leather satchel when he went to secondary school and when he turned eighteen we were going to take him to Rome. We'd also take him on the Orient Express one day because he liked trains so much, and we'd fly kites with him and play football and go paragliding.

One thing I didn't share with Mark was the day I found Kito in front of the mirror, wearing one of my dresses. He wasn't just dressing up for the fun of it, it was more serious than that. The way he was admiring himself in the mirror, trying to keep his improvised breasts in place. I watched him for a long time, without him noticing I was there. The dress looked good on him, I saw involuntarily, better than the stiff trousers he normally wore. He was a lot more graceful when he thought no one was looking; he was seducing himself in the mirror.

'Kito?' I asked, finally.

My voice made him start, he turned round like I'd caught him out. 'Why are you wearing a dress?'

He shrugged and started to tug at the dress, like he'd got himself entangled in it by accident.

'I just think it looks nice.'

He was his clumsy self again, plucking at the shoulder straps and looking at the ground.

'Take that thing off,' I said, and my voice sounded hoarse. 'Don't be silly.'

There was no answer.

'Take it off, go on. I'll make tea.'

Maybe a different kind of woman would have found the right words, struck the right tone; maybe I shouldn't have asked him anything about it. I looked at my son and thought of first times and mother-and-daughter things, as the magazines called it: first bra, first period, first boyfriend. The mothers were always pictured with their arms around their daughter, preferably in the same clothes, smiling the same open-mouthed smile.

When my first period arrived I didn't know what the red stains meant. I tried to wash them out and when that didn't work I threw the underpants away, in a bin outside. Much later I found myself squatting in a ditch with my mother, my period suddenly coming while we were on our way to visit relatives. I was desperately trying to insert a tampon. My mother had always thought me too young to use them before, which meant the blood sometimes seeped through my trousers during class, making me afraid to stand up. Becoming a woman was like being wounded, the sanitary towels like bandages.

'Just push it in, will you?' my mother hissed, looking to see if anyone was coming. 'Stop messing about.'

But my muscles were tense and rigid, which made it feel like I was pushing the tampon up against a wall. In the end my mother did it, pushing it in forcefully until the wall inside me disappeared and the only thing left was dull pain.

'You always make everything so difficult,' she said, standing up and brushing some grass off her skirt. She sat back down behind the wheel, waiting for me to resume my role as map-reader. 'It's not a big deal, you know.'

It was around that time I started to long for something soft. It didn't have to be a person, an animal would be fine, better maybe. A dog or cat, as long as it had a supple body, content to curl up against me. We never got a pet and it was only much later that I started dreaming of a baby, a little creature that would nurse at my breast, nestling in the curves of my body, feeling at home on the swell of my stomach. When it didn't arrive it left a hole inside me, giving a name to what I'd always known, that there was something dark and corrupted and hostile inside me.

Barren.

'It's not your fault,' Mark said, but his needing to say it at all proved it was my fault. It was through Mark's efforts we were able to adopt a child, his trust kept the process going. That's what everyone called it, the process.

That word masked the humiliation involved, the lengths we had to go to be considered suitable parents, while all I could do was wait for the question they never asked: why does your body destroy your children even before they have formed? What does that tell you about your suitability as a mother? And sure enough, towards the end of the process they turned out to have greater confidence in Mark than in me; my lack of openness worried them.

'I'll have the tea ready when you come down,' I told Kito, who'd started to take the dress off. The lipstick had left red smudges on his face, making him look like he'd been cut up. When he came down later he'd scrubbed his face and his cheeks were redder than usual.

'We love you – you know that, don't you?' I said, pouring him a cup of tea.

He stared at me. Every time we told him we loved him he'd turn his head away, like we'd slapped him.

'For a long time I thought I was a bad mother,' I said to Hannah. 'Too hard.'

We are sitting at the table, a pile of walnuts between us. We pull off the dark, tender fibres so the nuts

89

won't start rotting. The flesh stains our fingers like ink, impossible to wash off.

'But years ago I saw a bronze sculpture of a spider, huge and terrifying. The artist had intended it as an ode to her mother. After seeing that I thought maybe it's not such a bad thing, being hard, maybe it's just part of being a mother, being prepared to go to extremes to protect your child. It's impossible to understand when you don't have kids, the inventiveness and aggression you're capable of when necessary.

'He was such a sweet boy.

'But he never opened up, never ran the risk of showing us anything we might not approve of. Even later he would bring me flowers but he would never, ever, get angry. Sometimes I hoped he would, hoped he would give me that gift. There can't be many mothers who wish for something like that, but sometimes I wanted to shake him because when it came down to it he didn't trust us, not really. Even when he drew pictures for us, leaving them on our bed as presents, even then I wondered why, if maybe he wasn't sure we loved him, and how we could show him we did.

'So you have your doubts, and you buy baby alarms and car seats and my first phonics books and God knows what else. Thinking buying stuff will keep the danger away. Despite everything, you think you can do that.'

Silence.

Hannah looks at me from a distance, watching from across the table as I collapse, slumping down onto the ground. The armour that has been holding me together all this time is gone. I am defenceless, unable to keep myself upright. The woman I used to be would have disapproved of my weakness, the way I'm wailing like a run-over dog. But that woman is gone.

I'm already lying on the ground, small now, when Hannah comes over to me. She wraps a blanket round me and sits behind me, rubbing my back. 'You poor thing,' she says softly. 'You poor thing.'

Then, suddenly, it's over.

What am I doing here, why am I sitting here, why am I letting this woman touch me?

I push her away and get up, clumsily, abruptly. The blanket falls from my drawn up shoulders, uncovering my back, which now feels stiff and lifeless, like it's made of stone. It's what you do after a crying fit that matters. The way you wipe away your tears and blow your nose, ashamed, wanting to keep your eyes closed because it seems the best way to escape the moment. Weak and unsightly as the crying was in itself, the moment after you're already regretting the intimacy you have created by being so vulnerable, with the other person bending towards you and keeping her eyes on you, while you try and think of something, a joke, an observation, anything to restore you to your previous, adult self.

I go outside and walk through the back of the garden and up the hill, going beyond the walnut trees to a spot where the hedges haven't been trimmed and I am invisible. After a while, I don't know how long, she comes out too. 'Are you there?'

In the dark her voice sounds questioning, fragile. I stay outside until I can't keep my teeth from chattering, long after the lights in the house have gone out.

The next morning it's like nothing has happened. Hannah puts the kettle on without a word, wishes me a surly good morning as she hands me a cup of coffee, then huddles behind her own mug of tea. After breakfast we both seek out our own tasks. I wait for the moment she'll start asking questions – what his name was, where we lived – but she doesn't.

But later during lunch, to my own astonishment, I start talking again. 'My father died young, when I was still a child. And when we went to visit the grave (we never said we were visiting him, it was always "the grave", as if it was a person) it always surprised me how the gravestones around him were crooked and weathered, some of them broken, others overgrown, while Daddy's stone was always the same, the pink marble gleaming almost obscenely. When I was little I thought the state of the gravestone depended on the person lying underneath and whether they'd lived a good life.'

Hannah's picking at her nails. 'Have you seen the cemetery here?'

'I didn't know there was one.'

'It's worth seeing, very different to what we're used to.'

'In what way?'

She shrugs. 'You'll come across it, I'm sure.'

Because I've made a habit of going for a walk in the evenings after work, heading for the woods or through the village to the stream, where the water makes the air smell different. Sometimes I can't stand being in the same house with her anymore. And hardest of all is not knowing how long it'll take for her to start talking.

Not knowing if she'll ever tell me anything. And what then? When do I leave? Or should I trust what those kids told me and take my revenge anyway, even if I don't know exactly what for. The worst thing of all is that I can't hate her, not all the time, not while we're sharing this small space. Because the longer we do, the more difficult it becomes to see her as an abstraction I must destroy.

Being here is unnatural. Somehow I never considered what it would be like to accept her food and her honesty. I thought about it, sure, but I never felt anything. Now I'm here I'm disgusted, not just by her but by myself too, but despite that I can't stop this.

'What did he die of, your father?'

'A heart attack, when I was three. During the Olympics or one of the other events he used to watch in summer. A congenital defect, the doctor said, too much excitement maybe. Once a month, on a Sunday, we would visit my grandmother on my father's side, who served us tea and cinnamon biscuits and would cry as she watched me eat them. She always cried, the whole time we were there, whimpering even as she saw me out. That's where the photographs were: my father in yellowish hues; my parents cutting a wedding cake, their faces pale; my father as a boy, the books that used to belong to him. After one of those Sundays spent holding my breath I always felt an urge to do something crazy, like shouting in the middle of the street or taking my clothes off, it didn't matter what, as long as I felt alive, because every time it was like I'd escaped some kind of danger, infecting me, clinging to me like my grandmother's bony hand.

'He was an only child, your dad,' my mother would say, 'and that's why you should be careful too.' Every morning when I went to school she stood there on the garden path, saying 'I love you, I love you, I love you.' It sounded monotonous, like the repetitive call of a bird. She died many years ago, but there's still something inside me that strains to hear those words.

'Do you miss her?'

'I never got to know her properly, never got to see who she was, what she hoped for, what she dreamed of at night. I don't know if she grieved for my father, if she really missed him. At some point, we started lighting sky lanterns on the anniversary of his death. My mother wanted it, I don't know why. It wasn't the kind of gesture we went in for, I think it was just because those lanterns were popular. We lit one of those things in the park and watched it float into the air. My mother started walking, following until it disappeared behind a tree. She called out to me from a distance. "Can you see it?" I called back that I couldn't and then we went inside and had coffee, and that was that.'

My indifference is fake. What I'm really thinking is what a luxury it is to be able to sneer at funerals and rituals. Kito has a grave, he does now, but the body we lowered into it wasn't a body anymore, didn't have any muscle or substance. Because he'd been reduced to little more than his bones he belonged to the experts, the forensic dentist, the police, the people equipped to give him back his name based on those meagre remains. I wouldn't have recognized him if I'd found him myself – the curve of his nose, the dimples in his cheeks, his cheeks themselves: all gone.

Slowly, the air becomes colder. In the winter, Hannah says, there'll be nothing to do. 'If you're still here then we'll be holed up together.'

I try to discern emotion in her words, a tone of disapproval or satisfaction, but find nothing.

There are still a few warm, sunny days, almost like summer in their abundance, although the nights are chilly, the skies strewn with stars, the whole Milky Way visible. She says, 'The winter will arrive, it always does. Sometimes it's a little earlier or later but never that much. You can rely on the seasons here – you can die of heat or cold here, but at least you know what to expect.'

The skin of my hands has become rough. There are callouses on my fingertips, my palms, all the places where I've gripped the tools. Very slowly I am becoming tougher and better equipped. We use old-fashioned farming tools like the *kosa*, a scythe, to cut down the weeds on the edges of the field, and the *motika* to hack open and scrape away the earth. 'The Bulgarians laugh at us foreigners,' Hannah says, raising her hand to greet a man driving by in a combine harvester. 'They laugh, but they don't know what they're on the point of losing. There so much here that's still unspoilt.'

Each of those tools, the *kosa*, the *motika* and the *teslá*, each of them could easily be used to kill a person. The blades are razor-sharp, I feel the weight of the iron in my hand and even the wooden handles could be used to fracture a skull. Sometimes I look at them, trying to imagine how I'd approach her with one of these instruments. Maybe while she's sleeping or in another unguarded, unsuspecting moment. I picture the expression on her face changing, surprised at first and then – what? – indignant maybe, but not for long. But the images I conjure up are from TV programmes, they're not real, or not mine anyway. It would be simpler to suffocate her with a pillow. And Hannah herself has pointed out the hemlock that grows everywhere here in spring and is easily confused with edible plants. A fatal mistake, a painful death. An accident.

I don't know how to kill someone. How do you go about it, how do you gather the courage? Do you decide one morning that this is the day, or is it something that has to come over you? Or maybe it needs to grow, maybe you carry it around inside you long before you actually do the deed, and perhaps the final blow or thrust or jab isn't that important, not as important as all the times you pictured it, replaying it in your mind.

Sometimes I'm not sure I can stay here, if I'm capable of carrying out the plan I have conceived, to bring it to term.

Before winter starts, I will decide.

But where else can I go? Where else will I find a reason to get up in the morning? Hate is a beautiful thing, it's clear and sharp and the only thing I can still believe in, the only thing I can follow and understand. After his death, the hate grew in my belly; for the first time, I carried him in my body.

Hannah hold her hands up, the fingers stained black with the juice of the walnuts. She washes them, unsuccessfully, under the ice-cold water of the outside tap. She stretches out her arms in front of her and, staring in the middle distance, she declaims, 'Here's the smell of the blood still. All the perfumes of Arabia will not sweeten this little hand. Oh, oh, oh!'

Before I can say anything she takes a bow, introducing herself: 'Lady Macbeth, murderess.' When there's no reaction from me she adds, her voice much softer now, 'What's done cannot be undone.'

I nod, not capable of anything else, and then flee. Even from a distance I can smell the *rakia* on her breath.

The dog often escapes from its improvised kennel in the garden, staying away for days. The animal and I still look at each other with undisguised mistrust, though I do my best to hide that from Hannah.

I say, 'Come on, doggy, good girl.' Then she growls at me, and Hannah gives her a smack.

She doesn't tell me not to stroke the dog, she just watches.

'If she runs away in wintertime she'll die of cold, or someone will shoot her when they find her on their land. That's what happens here with stray animals, it's perfectly normal.' (But whenever the dog has gone off again she's always looking for it and calling it constantly, and when she thinks I'm not looking she rubs her hands through its fluffy coat and puts her arms around its neck. When she does that the dog starts drooling, lifting its head and nuzzling Hannah's legs.)

We stare at the empty kennel.

'This is a tough country,' Hannah says, 'it's not forgiving, not to anyone. It can't afford to be, and you need to adapt to that.'

'Why did you come here?' I ask.

She shrugs, and then carries on like she didn't hear me. 'In summer, even the trees struggle to survive in the drought and forty-degree heat. By the end, everything is withered. In winter the temperature can drop to minus twenty, the snow piling up metres high. If you don't have enough wood, there's a real chance you'll freeze to death. This country, it's harshness, it does something to people. Not the Bulgarians, they're used to it. But us Westerners, the ones who come here, to escape perhaps – we have no idea.'

'Why does someone your age choose to live here, so far away from everything?'

Something, I'm not quite sure what, in her face or body language maybe, tells me she's happy I've asked her this question, as if she's been waiting for someone to ask it for a long time; she still doesn't answer though. 'It's lonely here, although you don't notice that at first. When you've just got here, the loneliness seems like freedom. The way people here, we, the Westerners I mean, live – partying, slaughtering animals, buying horses and carriages – you'd think we've really broken away, that we're truly free. But once you're here, you find out who you really are, even if you'd prefer not to. That's what it means, being off the grid.'

Before I can ask another question, she stands up and shouts at the dog, who's coming out of the bushes with its tail between its legs.

After a couple of unexpectedly warm days she suggests going away. For a moment I think she's asking me to leave. But instead she says, 'There's a monastery not far from here, we can go there by car.'

I nod, unable to refuse, though I don't know what I'd want to go to a monastery for, on my own or with her. But as we pack our things I realize that it is an outing of sorts, a chance to go somewhere, a break from the daily routine.

I watch her as we climb the mountain near the monastery: her slight body under the loose fabric, the ease with which she picks her way among the stones.

'Do you believe in anything yourself?' I ask when we sit down to rest. Her pace is faster than mine, and it's only now we've stopped that I notice I'm breathing heavily and try to hide it. 'This place, I mean.'

'The religion here is too complicated for me, it's full of rules I don't understand. No, if I was religious I'd be an extremist. But I was searching for a long time.'

She takes some bread out of her backpack and takes a bite. 'Surrendering yourself, that's what attracts me. Giving yourself up to something completely.'

'Is that why you came here?'

Nearby, a bird flies up suddenly, its alarm call a shrill sequence of sounds.

'Maybe,' Hannah says. 'Maybe it was.'

I wait, but she doesn't continue. For a while the only sound is that of our chewing and the water far below.

She says, 'I used to have pictures from newspapers of horrible things hanging on the walls of my bedroom – a disturbed man beaten to death by the police, an emaciated child beside a bird waiting for him to die – I kept those photos there to remind me these things existed, were happening somewhere every day. I looked at them when I got up and before I went to bed, just stood there and looked. I had to make a real effort not to get used to them, to make sure I kept really seeing them. I thought those pictures would work like an inoculation, helping me to do the right thing, stopping me from looking away and becoming indifferent.'

'But now you're here. Far away from the world.'

'I told you, it was hard. It isn't pleasant looking at those things.' She sounds annoyed. 'Why did you become a psychiatrist? Did you want to help people?'

I kick away a stone. 'My mother wanted me to go into cardiology, to help people with heart problems.'

'But what did you want?'

'There are people who become psychiatrists because they want to help people, really sympathize with them. There are others who just aren't good enough for other specializations, or think psychiatry is where they can do the least damage. And then there are people who are resistant to unhappiness, capable of shaking off the drab corridors and hopelessness. That was the kind of person I was.

'These days people expect too much from suffering. We pretend despair is an exalted state that naturally confers insight and dignity. People who think that way have never seen the patients who pace the lino day in day out, hands shaking as they light cigarette after cigarette. They've never seen their despair when the medication that was supposed to help them takes away the very thing they see as their own self.'

'But why did you stay?'

'Maybe I didn't belong anywhere else.'

When she stands up soon after and walks on ahead her limp seems more pronounced, though it could just be my imagination. We're walking downhill now, towards a chapel whose walls are covered with icons. Beside it is the opening of a cave.

'At the end of that cave there's a hole. If you pass through it, all your sins are forgiven.'

She laughs.

I follow her through the cave, which is cold and damp, and wait as she clambers up, not offering to help. Neither does she hold out her hand as I struggle through the hole and out into the open, where, suddenly, there is the sound of birds, and sunlight filtered through bright green leaves. 'You can make a wish now,' she says, pointing to a wall behind us.

Hundreds of bits of paper have been jammed between the stones.

'I don't have wishes anymore.'

She shrugs, takes a piece of paper, scribbling something I can't read. She folds it into a wad and wedges it in one of the cracks, before walking off without a backward glance.

'What did you wish for?'

'If I tell you it's sure not to come true.'

The monastery's not like I imagined, it's more colourful. Apart from the monks that is, who wear black robes and walk more quickly and purposefully than the visitors. On one gallery, washing has been hung out to dry among the geraniums. I admire the murals on the walls and vaulted ceilings – the artist hasn't used perspective and this makes the images more primitive but also more direct than the paintings I'm used to seeing at home. At a stall I buy a postcard with a weeping woman, Mary I presume, her face drawn and her hands folded. The reverse is completely blank. Now and then, I take it out and try to think of something to write to Mark. I get out my pen a few times, only to put it back, because the empty space is more eloquent than anything I could say or ask. In all the pictures of Mary, it looks like she's not really holding her child. She's displaying him, offering him up; she's giving him to the world that is going to kill him. In the church, where old women are praying, I don't know where to stand – the space doesn't have any clear demarcations showing what part is holy and off limits. I look at Hannah from the corner of my eye, but her eyes are closed. I wonder if she's praying and later, when she lights a candle, I wonder who she's lighting it for.

There are other, smaller outings. To a market in a neighbouring town. There, I notice how much I've grown used to the silence of the village. Although it isn't large, the town tires me out. When he was little, I used to take Kito to the market, and he'd be given something to eat at nearly every stall. He ate a lot in those days, like he was making up for his time in the orphanage and was never quite sure he'd be allowed to keep the banana or piece of cheese, so he wolfed them down. Despite this, all the market traders looked at him with the special affection reserved for children. Only then did they turn to me, with a look of surprise. At that age he didn't understand how those things worked, didn't even notice the difference in skin colour. But everyone else was surprised I was Kito's mother. It always took a while before they realized we belonged together, and at that moment I always saw the same expression move across their faces; a brief moment of shock and then a conscious decision to find it perfectly normal.

I couldn't have imagined beforehand that adoption was such a taboo, and the simple fact that my child hadn't emerged from my womb, from my vagina, would be such an obstacle. Not just for all those people who hardly knew us but also, repeatedly, for me. Because you don't say, never say, 'You're not my child', but sometimes you do think it, even though you don't want to. The only reason you're thinking it is because you know you shouldn't. And because he's thinking it too, whenever there's an argument, thinking the thing he can't, mustn't, ever say: 'You're not my real mother.' You're constantly afraid he'll say it, that he might be thinking it that very moment.

'When you own land,' Hannah says, as we wander past the stalls, 'and know how to work it, you're not dependent on anyone.'

We've harvested pumpkins, cucumbers, tomatoes, corn. There's the fruit from the trees – peaches, apples, pears and cherries. We eat as much as we can, then start making preserves. For days on end, there are pans of boiling water in the garden. Sometimes one of the *babas* passes by and nods approvingly. We give any fruit that's left over to the neighbours, who use it to make *rakia*. The mulberries are dried, to be used in baking later. But we're far from self-sufficient. Hannah battles with the land, against the weeds that keep coming back, against the drought, the insects that eat the roots that should be growing underground, and the rats. 'When you come here you think everything will be simple. The earth, the plants and your own hands and energy. But you need to learn how to do every single thing, even making a fire.'

Then she shrugs, wipes her hands on her already dirty jeans, and carries on. She stares at the gnawed roots she's just dug up, her face determined. She swears loudly when a chicken disappears without trace, or one of the plants shrivels or doesn't come up at all. And then she immediately starts on a new project, with renewed hope. She doesn't know the soil here; ultimately she's a city child, like me. The old women tell her what to do, shaking their heads at such ignorance, laughing at us as you would at children.

'Later,' Hannah says, 'I'll invite people round. I see a large table and all of us sitting round it, eating. We'll laugh and talk until it gets dark and we'll understand each other.'

Her arm sweeps across the empty field, sketching out the scene, the size of the table.

In the evening I call Mark, to tell him I'm fine, I'm alive, I'm well.

'When are you coming back?' he asks.

I don't answer, but ask him what he's doing now – we don't ask each other about feelings anymore, just about things that are relatively safe.

'When are you coming home?'

His voice is hoarse, and he swallows hard when I say goodbye. He deserves someone else, someone nicer. He deserves someone who isn't constantly reminding him of what he's lost. But if I stay here long enough, far away from everything, sooner or later he will forget me. He's already started to, even if he doesn't realize it, walking ahead while I stay in the same spot. Like that time when I was little, when I was in the dunes with my mother and we got into a fight, and I just stood there waiting out of pure bloody-mindedness, feeling the eyes of the trees in my back, their branches stretching into the sky like malevolent hands.

'One more party,' Hannah says. 'One more party before the winter starts.'

She seemed unhappy this past week, dissatisfied with the results of the harvest. I thought I could hear her crying at night; in the mornings her eyes were swollen and red. I asked no questions, felt no need to comfort her, just did what was expected of me, staying out of her way. Now she seems to have got over whatever it was; even her movements are different, more abrupt than during the past few days. She's suddenly switched to a state of feverish activity, getting up and rummaging in the storage cupboard, making preparations, covering the table with jars. Later she calls her friends. She sounds too enthusiastic, her laugh slightly artificial. It shocks me to realize I now know her well enough to judge this, and will always remember what she sounds like when she's hoping for something.

On the morning of the party we decorate the garden with coloured lights. For days we've been getting up early to make pastry, bake cakes, prepare vegetables. Hannah is nervous and almost childishly excited. 'Shaun's bringing round a goat later,' she says. 'We're having clay-baked goat tonight.' It's one of the autumn's last warm days.

I'm not really listening, chopping tomatoes and gherkins. I'm surprised when, a little later, Shaun – twenties, cut-off jeans, dark hair in a messy ponytail – walks into the garden with a live goat. Trailing behind them is a nervous woman about my age, her face hidden under an enormous sun hat.

Hannah explains: 'Shaun was a butcher back home and over here he's the one who slaughters the animals. For the foreigners, I mean.'

The goat belongs to the nervous woman, who looks on as Shaun sharpens his knife with calm, careful movements. I turn away while the animal is still alive, telling Hannah I'm going for a walk. She's busy talking to the woman, who has a loud, unpleasant voice.

'You go,' she says, pouring boiling water to make coffee, 'Tina will help me here.'

I follow the path down to the stream.

The last party I attended was one I organized for Kito. He didn't want it, but I insisted.

'Everyone likes parties. Just invite your classmates, they'll like that.'

'They won't come.'

'Of course they will. If you don't try anything they can't get to know you,' I told him.

I tried to catch his eye, but he turned away, fiddling with the strings of his hoodie. When he was at the age for musical chairs and pin the tail on the donkey, our garden was always full of Mark's nieces and nephews and kids from the neighbourhood. There were also the children we'd got to know during the adoption process, older now and looking different than in the videos, but still recognizable, and not just by the colour of their skin. It was as if the way they moved was slightly different to the rest, slightly less natural – or maybe I was just seeing what I expected to see. Either way, those parties had been a success, with children eating cake and blowing bubbles and the sound of their voices and laughter. Maybe that's what I was longing for when I insisted on a party, trying to recapture something that had disappeared all too quickly. I kept going on about it until he shrugged and said, 'Fine, if that's what you want.'

'It's for you, Kito. It'll be your party.'

He wasn't listening, he'd already walked away from me.

I asked him to invite his friends, his classmates. We'd lost touch with the children who used to come to his parties; the group of adoptive parents had long since fallen apart.

On the day of the party I baked two cakes and some quiches and decorated the house. I asked Kito again if he'd invited his classmates and he nodded sullenly.

Five o'clock came and went.

'The first ones will be arriving soon,' I said. And then it turned six, and then seven and eight.

We waited.

We stared at the cake, which was looking less and less appetizing, and at the phone. It didn't ring. Kito avoided our gaze.

'Someone's bound to come soon,' I said, my cheerfulness forced and too loud. From time to time Mark threw his hands up in the air. 'Now then,' he'd say, as if there was something that needed doing. Then he would look around the room and sink back in his chair.

107

I wished we hadn't given Kito his present in the morning; I wanted to give him something now. I wished so badly that I had something to give him, but I had nothing, and so I became angry. 'You didn't ask them, did you? If you'd invited them someone would have come.'

He didn't shout back or walk out of the room, just hunched down even more in his chair.

'I did ask them.'

Mark stood up suddenly. I tried to put an arm round Kito, but he moved away from me. Just to have something to do I started clearing up, putting the food in the fridge, before changing my mind and chucking it all in the bin – none of us would want to eat it now.

'Was that necessary?' Mark asked me later, when we were in bed, not touching.

'He needs friends, kids his age, he's so alone.'

'Do you think this is helping?'

'He needs to learn this kind of thing. To make contact.'

Mark sniffed loudly and we said nothing more. Maybe that's when we started moving apart from each other – that birthday, the cold silence of that day.

At this moment the goat is being slaughtered in Hannah's garden. Shaun is drawing the knife across the animal's throat in one supple movement. I picture its head pulled back to uncover the artery, blood starting to flow. Do goats cry out before they die? I walk along the stream, where the air smells fuller and heavier, past houses that are barely there anymore, their walls crumbling where the snow and rain has eaten away the loam. What used to be here has moved on, disappeared.

I climb the hill, my eyes fixed on the edge of the wood. Only when I look up do I realize I've reached the cemetery, randomly situated among some dry fields. The graves themselves are white and showy, monuments rather than simple stones, small houses complete with roofs. Some have marble benches beside them holding bottles of beer. One grave is newly dug, the earth loose, fresh flowers laid on top. I kneel down by the cross stuck into the earth and wait for something I can't give a name to. I wonder if people here gather round their dead, drinking to what used to be. Should I build a house for Kito, I ask myself; I'd like to believe in a place to go back to. I'd have preferred it if his body – or what was left of it, but you don't say remains, only the papers and police do that – I'd have preferred for it to have been burned. In the olden days they used to have funeral pyres, and sometimes the living would throw themselves onto them too. Back then they understood what grief was.

They hadn't shown up to his birthday, but they all came to his funeral. His classmates, his little round-shouldered friends. From a great distance I watched the grief they dared claim as theirs, the tears running down their cheeks. I had to supress an urge to touch those tears to see if they were real. Other mothers looked at me, at the creature I had become. I had lost my skin and turned into a small, bloody thing. It would be better if I stayed in the dark, where nobody could see me and nothing would touch me.

'I'm so sorry,' they said. 'So very sorry.'

I looked at them and said nothing. Their voices sounded hollow. They were sorry, but they were also relieved that it wasn't their child and maybe, later at the dinner table, they would say how you could never be sure with adopted children. Their words contained a vague reproach: how can you go on living with that, a dead child, when you failed to notice the signs?

An acquaintance of ours had seen Kito cycling, not long before he disappeared. He was laughing madly, or so she thought, cycling along on his own. I'd answered that you get that sometimes, private jokes can make you laugh like that, and she said, 'Yes, you get that at that age.' Now she'd sent us a card, telling us, in her neat hand, that she realized now he hadn't been laughing that time but must have been crying, 'crying so hard' that she couldn't get the image out of her head. They were so unashamed, pouring out their shock and sadness over me – how terrible it was, and there were no words to express, etc. – as if I cared what they felt.

Of course they all thought they'd do things differently, better. They were all wearing make-up and tailored black skirts and jackets. I was wearing a turtleneck jumper, the only item of clothing I could stand wearing then, pulling up the collar to hide half my face. All those people, they distracted me. All this was supposed to be about Kito, this was the last time I would ever take him anywhere.

Mark said some words, or tried to. He broke down at the third sentence and started weeping.

Everyone looked at him.

He stumbled through the words, his face open and defenceless. I didn't understand how he could expose himself like that. Apparently, the highly personal things he'd wanted to say could only be expressed in clichés.

How special Kito was. How lucky we'd been to get to know him. How we'd failed him.

Mark believed Kito had committed suicide and now that was what everyone thought. As the coffin was lowered into the ground, it started pouring down. Umbrellas went up and people huddled closer together, seeking shelter. I watched them but remained where I was. I stood by the edge of his grave, feeling the cold rain soaking my jumper. That's what it would be like from now on, little pieces of my son like shards of glass in my belly.

I get up with difficulty, dusting the sand off my knees. I stand there for a minute, as if waiting for some insight or revelation, but of course I feel nothing. Leaving the cemetery I see a small wooden shed I hadn't noticed before. The wooden cladding is covered in papers with photographs, names and dates, some half-faded. The dead stare at me, printed in black and white.

When I get back to Hannah's the goat has disappeared and Shaun is sweating. There are dark stains on the bare patch of ground on the other side of the yard.

'Where's the goat?' I ask, stupidly, and Hannah nods towards the fire.

The woman called Tina giggles. She's taken her sun hat off and is fanning herself. Now and then, while we talk, she lays her puffy hand amicably on Hannah's shoulder. Hannah doesn't react, but she doesn't move away either.

Slowly, the guests start to arrive. They're mostly foreigners who live in the villages around here. One old man wears a cowboy hat, his grey hair in thin braids.

There's a young guy with large, watery eyes who says he wants to do something for the animals here, another who's constantly smoking hash. A few couples, some of the women carrying babies on their arm, some older children as well. They'll stay awake till the end, running around, dancing with the adults and shouting, their voices becoming shriller the later it gets.

All the guests have brought food and the wooden tables are soon crowded with dishes. There's bread, stewed apples, pies and cakes, small fried fish, salads made of tomato, cucumber and feta, and corn on the cob, glistening with butter. Shaun stands beside the fire, occasionally poking the clay with a stick. Expectation builds as it gets darker and the temperature drops. There's a lot of drinking, and many toasts to Hannah. She laughs, raising her glass. I'm not drinking. I watch the women belly dancing, shawls tied around their waists, white flesh visible under their T-shirts and tops. A group of Bulgarian youths from the village have gathered. They stare at the women from a distance, their faces inscrutable.

The little girls act like grown-ups here, while the women act like children. Hannah joins the dancing, her slight body moving smoothly to the music. She dances the way an older woman might, longing for a time past. It's not her face, which remains frighteningly immobile, but her body itself that knows it isn't coming back, whatever it is. When she dances her limp is hardly noticeable. She must have learned long ago to conceal her bad leg. Tina comes and sits next to me and, bending towards me, she says, 'Back home I was always scared, isn't that strange?' She has a tic in her right eye.

It's only after I've been watching the dancing women for a while that I feel jealousy rising up. The utter lack of embarrassment, the shameless way they shake their buttocks, bellies and breasts. It looks ridiculous, of course. They've discarded all layers of perfection; they're dancing. They are beautiful only because they think themselves beautiful. They laugh, in themselves, at others, to each other, forming an uninhibited sisterhood I am not part of and must therefore despise. Because I am sitting here, watching, moving cautiously between people I don't understand. Again and again, I create an island around me – conversations falter when I try to join in, the rug I'm sitting on is gradually deserted as the people around me go in search of other, better company. I don't mind, I'm used to it. That one fact, his death, overpowers all other topics more suitable for conversations with strangers or even friends. At first I tried to tell people, repeating over and over what had happened, even though I didn't know myself.

But friends hoped for a change and my patients expected me to heal, expected someone to look up to. A woman whose son has disappeared, has died, is not perfect, nobody could claim that. So after a while I gave up hope that someone would understand me when I said 'My son is gone' or, later, 'He's dead.' I heard patients and friends talk about their grief, the things that made them furious or desperate. I'd listen vacantly, because what they called rage or desperation had nothing to do with what I felt anymore. The words have been hollowed out, a gulf has opened up between myself and the rest of the world. I'm used to it by now.

The only thing that surprises me is to see Hannah retreating from the party too, looking on as the others enjoy themselves. Only when someone calls out to say the goat's ready does she stand up, once again looking much older than she is. Everyone gathers round the fire. It's dark now and the fire casts shadows over our faces. A little boy takes Shaun's hunting knife from its sheath and hands it over reverentially. Someone's playing an African drum. Meanwhile, Shaun is freeing the goat from the fire pit as best he can, scraping the clay and ashes off the dead animal's skin. I force myself to look. Walking away would be a weakness and I can't permit myself any weaknesses, not anymore. Hannah has wrapped her arms round her body; this morning's childish enthusiasm seems to have disappeared. The others cheer as the goat is lifted awkwardly from the ashes. It is covered in charred patches and its neck dangles over the edge of the metal container the men have placed it in almost tenderly. I think of Kito, the way someone must have picked him up, carried him, his body powerless and already deserted. The victim.

Someone calls for water, but I don't move. I'm looking at the goat's lips, which are vulnerable and soft. As Shaun sticks the knife in and starts skinning the animal, before skilfully dividing it into chunks, a circle of people gathers round. Even the Bulgarian youths look impressed. It's a while before I notice Hannah has gone. No one else seems to notice.

I find her sitting under the apple tree at the top of the hill, leaning against the trunk with her arms wrapped round her knees. I expect her to send me away, but she says nothing when I squat down beside her. We look at

114

the people moving below us in the glow of the fire, and up at the cold stars.

'When I first came here,' Hannah says suddenly, 'before I'd bought this house, I stayed with a British woman. Her name's Caroline, she's here tonight.

'I came here after – after something had gone wrong. I came here with an entirely mistaken idea of what life would be like here. I looked forward to getting my hands dirty. We would work, make preserves, prepare the garden for winter – whatever that involved, it sounded good anyway. I'd be able to stay with Caroline indefinitely, but starting with a trial period of three weeks. After that, we would start looking for a house of my own, a house just the right size with some land. I'd be able to sow and then harvest whatever grew there. I'd be able to reap the fruits of the land and get up to see the dew on the grass. I would eat what was available.

'I had a feeling something deep inside me was sick, weakened.

'I thought maybe it was the food flown in from thousands of kilometres away, or the constant bombardment of advertising messages that were making me feel so vulnerable, so dependent. Or perhaps it was the rays from the microwave or the Wi-Fi or the telephone, or simply having all those devices around. Maybe, if I could live off the land, I would get better, become stronger. Maybe it had got into my cells.

'We looked at houses. So many broken fragments of lives, so much driftwood – fallen chunks of plaster, books, tools, balls of wool and pieces of fabric, photos, medicine bottles, and that was only what I saw at first glance. The serious faces in the photographs, children's handwriting; why had all those things been gathered so carefully only to be left behind so carelessly? Someone must have formed those letters laboriously, must have taken those pictures. It was like those families had never left.

'Those were the kind of thoughts I had and I felt lost. And then Caroline would call out from the garden, "This vine here, that's worth something. It must be dozens of years old. Here. Taste this." She would hand me some grapes and she was right, they were sweet and full of flavour and we'd munch on them as the Bulgarian owner looked on smilingly, hopefully. Sometimes I think the only reason I bought this house was the taste of the grapes.'

'There are worse reasons.'

'That's true.' She breathes out, and says, 'The vine here, the thick one near the house, that's more than just a plant. When I think of all the years it takes for a vine to grow that size, how they must have carefully trained it years ago to grow upwards to provide the shelter and grapes it still does today, or even just what it takes to survive the winters here. That vine is the soul of this place. If it wasn't there you couldn't sit outside in summer. I look at it when I wake up. I don't know what I'd do if it ever died.'

Rarely have I heard this much emotion in her voice. Only someone who has withdrawn into herself completely could think this way, worrying about a plant, letting the death of a child pass by unnoticed.

'What was it like?' I ask. 'Arriving here? What was it like when you first came here?'

'The air was different, I remember that. Fuller, heavy with the scent of flowers and hay and animals, or some combination like that – I knew nothing then, didn't even know the difference between hay and straw. But this was the place, I knew that. This was where I would arrive and stay and become happy, someone with feeling in my fingers and strength in my hands.'

But that never happened, I think. If it had worked, she'd be down there now with all the others, who are broken too, perhaps, but are carrying on with the party at least, carrying on and having children. Instead, she's sitting here in the dark with me. So reluctant to face the company of the people she calls her friends that she's left the warmth of the fire. Or was it the goat, the butchered animal she couldn't bear, even though she'd been looking forward to it so much?

'It was strange, coming here. There was a man waiting for me at the airport, holding my name in his hands. Just someone from the hostel, but I'd never been met at an airport before and I was moved that there was someone waiting for me. He insisted on carrying my bags and asked me what the weather was like in Holland, and I had no idea. He pointed to the taxi drivers – 'you can't trust them' – and I remember nodding, saying that was one thing which was the same everywhere you went, but he said that no, everything was worse here and I felt I'd been put in my place. Despite that, he nodded at me in a friendly, patient way. I put my seatbelt on and looked straight ahead as he paid and drove out of the car park. It's not that I didn't want to talk to him but I didn't know what to say. I asked what he did for a living. I don't know anything about cars, but the smooth

117

motion and white-leather upholstery of this one told me it was expensive.

'He said he was employed as a Balkans specialist by a member of the US congress. Next week he'd be leaving for Washington again, and then on to Dubai – had I ever been to Dubai? he asked. No, I told him, I'd never been, because I'd never been anywhere. He kept talking, about Bulgaria's many springs – 'springs are our biggest capital' – while I stared out the window. What I saw put me in mind of a third-world country, it had none of the purity I'd hoped for. But then you know what it looks like yourself.

'"On holiday?" he asked and I nodded, holidays, yes, because how do you tell a man like that you want to start a new life here? It would sound childish, immature, typical for someone from a rich country who has had all their chances and wasted them. "In Bulgaria we start over again every fifty years," he said, and for a moment I was confused, but he was talking about laws, political systems. "Every fifty years we try a new system, it's always tomorrow here. For Bulgarians it's always going to happen tomorrow, always," he said, as he dropped me outside the hostel, lifting my backpack out of the boot.

'I watched as the car drove off and felt deserted, the heat building up walls of air the moment I moved. On the other side of the street an old man was cleaning his car with a corner of a rag, going about it more meticulously than I'd ever seen. Further along, a group of youngsters standing round a motorbike were looking at me, blatantly staring.

'Later, in my room, I lay awake, listening to the sound of the ventilators. This is it, I thought. This has to be it.

Even saying it out loud couldn't help me drown out my own disappointment. I'd withdrawn all my money, had come here on an impulse, because I happened to read an article the week before about foreigners who were coming to repopulate the villages here. From Sofia, I emailed the people in the article. Two of them had a website, they sold houses themselves. Caroline was the first to respond, writing that I was welcome to stay and how best to get to her place: seven hours in the train plus a taxi ride. I remember how small I felt in the main hall of the train station in Sofia – you haven't seen it, but it's one of those old-fashioned communist-era buildings. Old men kept coming up to me, offering to buy me a ticket or show me the way to the platform. I didn't know whether they were being friendly or trying to take advantage of me, my disability or my ignorance.

'Coming here was the furthest I dared, although the kids I used to teach were always talking about Morocco, South Africa, India and Australia. They mentioned those places so casually, like they were just round the corner. I have met people here who are no longer able to settle, who get restless and eventually leave again, time after time. I'm a bad traveller, though, it makes me nervous. Even while packing I'm scared I'll forget something; I'm not cavalier enough to believe in the mantra that all you need is your passport and a credit card. It isn't true anyway, that isn't me staring out at me from my passport ("That's the best we can do," the photographer had said with a shrug). I'm not myself without all the things I leave behind at home, I feel robbed of something even before I've left the house.

'Now I've got here I'm not leaving, I'm done with travelling. I won't force myself into a mould that doesn't fit me, not again. Sitting in that station, feeling so small, was the first time I could start to see an opening, a space from which I could carry on after everything had ground to a halt back home. "Here," I said, "I am here now. I am the person walking here." But as I said it I stumbled over a hole in the pavement – I almost fell and had to grab hold of something. The city was too large, too fast and too hot, and there were too many cars driving too quickly. I wandered through the streets of Sofia without stopping, except now and then to stare at stray dogs in the distance. I tried not to walk too quickly, because there was nowhere I needed to get to. But my legs kept upping the tempo automatically because it was easier to become one of the crowd, pretending to be just another commuter, instead of keeping to the leaden, slow rhythm of relaxation, of just being. Later, when I was tired enough to sit down outside a cafe, I watched gigantic marble heads being removed from a museum and loaded into a van, the proud noses of emperors and heads of state, their sharp profiles powerless, at the mercy of the hands carrying them. A chubby, blonde little girl was rocking herself to and fro on a bench near the cafe, trying every so often to catch the attention of her mother, who never looked up, intent on her telephone conversation. The statues in the park looked caring somehow.

'In the evening I noticed I'd left the light on in my room. The floor was covered with dozens of moths, powerless, dashed to pieces. I tried to pick one up but its wing was stuck to the floor. Their bodies were so soft it almost made me want to stroke them, and that made me cry. You have to understand, I was very weak then. Wounded, you could say.'

'I don't understand,' I said. 'What had happened, what could have hurt someone your age so badly?'

She doesn't answer my question. When she starts talking again she sounds deep in thought, like she's forgotten I'm sitting next to her.

'I was young then, I mean not like I am now but softer, stupider, I didn't understand how things worked. I didn't want to teach but it was what I was doing. Children need someone they can believe in; I didn't even believe in myself.

'I'd repeat things to myself in the mornings when I got up, quotes from the internet. I had a list with a hundred things I wanted to do that year. I did yoga. I took care of myself. I wanted to recapture the feeling I had when I decided to go to drama school, the sense of possibility. Suddenly I was older than I thought. Looking in the mirror I could see the woman I would become, how tired she'd be. People my age had cars, partners – children, some of them. They made choices I couldn't understand. I waited. I felt a strong desire to give, but I didn't know what I had to give. I wanted people to expect something of me.

'The subject I taught was pointless, a time-filler. No one expected it to be more than that, a box to be ticked, a line in the school prospectus.

'It was my third supply job in two years, my failure was almost complete. I tried too hard, that was the problem. At my last school the pupils spoke to each other in Arabic so I wouldn't understand. At the school before that a girl with a real talent for acting said her parents would never allow her to do something like that because acting was for whores. "This is a bad school," the pupils said. "What's the point of doing our best at a bad school?" I said that my lessons were about them, but they just laughed at me. "Why should we do our best for a subject that's no use to anyone?" I couldn't cope with that level of cynicism. This school was my last chance, and they only took me on because a friend, Maureen, recommended me. We'd known each other for a long time, then – I haven't spoken to her in ages now. But that's the way things go.'

Suddenly she sounds curt and I am afraid she's going to stop even before she's started her story. Minutes go by while we sit there in silence.

'They needed a substitute for drama at the school where Maureen worked, because the regular teacher was off with stress. After my interview I looked him up on the class photos and saw a grey, tired-looking man, who seemed to keep himself apart even from his own form. No wonder he didn't make it, I thought. I was convinced I'd do things differently. I'd become a confidante for the pupils, an inspiring example like teachers in films. But of course I wasn't that kind of teacher, I never had been. That had become clear during my placements as a student. You either have it or you don't, and in those first, difficult weeks some of my colleagues patted me on the back and said – by way of encouragement, although it was hardly encouraging – that maybe I was just too young. "Things might have been different if you were a man." I didn't really listen to their advice but I nodded, passively. Clearly everybody knew how difficult I was finding it.

'That first day I was three-quarters of an hour early. I had spent almost a week preparing my lesson. While I was moving the tables and chairs aside the deputy headmaster, Van Eeteren, tapped on the window: "You putting all that back at end of the lesson? We've got another homework club here this afternoon and I don't want any arguments between the teachers. What's on the programme anyway?"

'"*Richard III*."

'No secondary school pupil would light up at the mention of Shakespeare – I could have picked something else, something simpler. "I know it might sound pretentious, but I'm convinced that if we take the pupils seriously, they will do the same with us – we need to appeal to them at a higher level if we really want to get a response and I have already thought about how I—"

'I believed in what I said, I did in those days. But he interrupted me, "I meant, what class?"

'"4D."

'He sucked in his cheeks. "Well, I have to tell you that form's known as the Class from Hell."

'When he saw my face he said, "Kidding, I'm kidding. They're not easy, but as I understand it everything will turn out all right if you appeal to them at a higher level. Well, good luck later and see you around."

'He walked off, his shoes squeaking on the linoleum. Quarter of an hour before the start of my first class and I'd already made my first enemy. I went back to my desk, rearranging the papers I'd arranged once already.

I looked for a place to stand where my leg wouldn't be too noticeable. Repeated to myself what I was going to say. The first lesson is crucial, it's the deciding moment, when the class judges who's stronger, whether you're a suitable prey.

'I took out my hair band, letting my hair down.

'I tied it back again, loosening one lock.

'I untied it again.

'I repeated the way I would start the class, yet again. "Is there a murderer here?" I would ask. "No. Yes, I am." Once I'd caught their attention I'd talk about Richard III, the villain, outsider and unfortunate wretch. "Is there a murderer here?"

'They came in slowly, one by one, dragging their feet, like condemned prisoners to the scaffold. A girl with heavily made-up eyes in a pale face. A boy in skate pants, a chain hanging out on one side. A blonde girl with a ponytail and a bored expression.

'A black kid who shuffled in, his eyes glued to the floor.'

It's strange, but when I hear Hannah describing Kito, I start to laugh. I've imagined this moment, or tried to at least, and how I'd keep my face impassive while she talked about him. But obviously there was no way I could prepare for this, not on my own.

I don't know why I'm laughing; I can think of more logical reactions.

But this is what happens, nervous laughter that threatens to tip over into tears, making Hannah look at me strangely, almost concerned.

I force myself to calm down, pressing my nails so deeply into my skin that the red, crescent-shaped marks remain visible for days afterwards.

'Did you think that was funny?' she asks, irritated.

'I've had too much to drink.'

When she doesn't carry on, I say 'I'm sorry, I'm not good with alcohol.'

She doesn't need much encouragement.

'There was also a tall, skinny boy wearing a baseball cap. Van Eeteren had drummed it into me that baseball caps were not allowed in class: "If we allow those, who knows where it'll end." So I had to say something. I should have rehearsed it, found a way of saying it that was friendly but not condescending, strict but not too strict.

'"You'll take your cap off, won't you?" I asked.

'I knew immediately it had been the wrong thing to say. It had sounded questioning instead of authoritative, and the boy paused, standing right in front of me. He was tall enough to look down on me and he waited a few seconds before replying, with exaggerated politeness, "Of course, Miss."

'But he didn't take it off and I didn't say anything more. I'd save it for later, I told myself; this isn't the moment to make a big deal out of it.

'Not finding their chairs in the usual position, the students stopped in their tracks. They crowded together at the edge of the classroom, staring at my leg.

'"Sit down," I said, "sit down."

'But they didn't sit down. They looked at each other, the girls giggling. They got out their phones.

'"Sit down," I said again. And then, leading by example, I sat down on the floor. That was a mistake as well, as the students were now towering above me. I got up again.

'"Sitting or standing, what's it supposed to be?" the tall, skinny boy asked.

'"I'm not sitting on the floor," the blonde girl said. "Do you know how filthy this place is?"

'I hesitated.

'"All right then. Move the tables back, but leave some space in the front where we can play."

'"Oh," the boy in the cap said, "we're going to play are we? Kinky."

'"Take your cap off."

'To my surprise, he did, and maybe that was the signal the others had been waiting for. They started moving the tables and chairs. They're scared too, I thought, when something unexpected happens and the natural order is disrupted. They're like old people in that sense.

'Finally, they were sitting down. The way in which they'd distributed themselves through the classroom was an exact representation of the hierarchy among the students, but I didn't know that yet. The tall, thin boy sat at the back, slouching in his chair, and all the others kept looking at him. To the side sat a group of giggling girls, their heads bent towards each other over the table. Ponytail girl sat next to a girl with an equally blonde ponytail, looking expectant. The girl with the heavily made-up eyes was drawing a skull in her notebook. The black boy sat on his own.

'I waited for them to quieten down, but that didn't happen.

'"Lower your voice," it says in the training manuals, "and the students will have to do their best to listen."

'I cleared my throat and said, softly, "Right, I'd like to start now."

'The noise the students were producing didn't let up one bit. It was like they hadn't noticed me.

'Like a storm, I thought. Or maybe there's a storm brewing and that's why they're like this, maybe they're at the mercy of something else. I started again, more loudly now. "I want to start with a round of names. I'm very keen to know who you are and maybe you'd like to know who I am too."

'"I don't feel well," the blonde girl said. "Can I go outside?"

'"What's wrong with you?" I asked.

'"You really want me to discuss it in front of the whole class?"

'When I got back to the classroom all the chalk had disappeared. I checked the container under the blackboard. Then the desk. I was certain there had been some, I'd made sure beforehand. There was sniggering from the class.

'"Missing something?" the tall, skinny boy asked. He'd put his cap back on. A strand of his hair was plastered against his forehead with hair gel.

'"Yes." I looked around. The sniggering became louder. I couldn't see a piece of chalk anywhere. The skinny boy – I still didn't know his name – started laughing. I suddenly thought of nature documentaries, of hyenas cornering gazelle, slowly, inevitably, deadly.

'"Is this what you're looking for?"

'Something landed beside me on the floor. I bent down to pick up the piece of chalk.

'"Lovely pair of knickers," the boy drawled.

'My hand shot to my dress involuntarily.

'"Yes, they're the ones I mean."

'I knew I had to send him out, right then, that minute. Had to show him he'd gone too far. Or, if I'd been someone else, a man or just older and more experienced, I could have put him in his place with a joke. But I didn't have enough front, didn't have the voice to take him on. I turned to the board to hide my face. "Never turn your back on the class, that way you lose them instantly." That was the first thing I'd learned, but all I felt like doing now was getting out of the classroom, and when I spoke again it was in a bright tone that sounded false even to myself.

'"My name is Hannah. I am here to teach you drama."

'The skinny boy yawned ostentatiously. Another opportunity to put him in his place, but I ignored it, laughing submissively like he'd made a joke. "It's not that bad, you'll see."

'"Will I?" he asked. "Will I see that, *Hannah*?"

'Earlier I had quarrelled with Van Eeteren because I didn't want the students to use my last name like they did with all the other teachers. That way we'll never get the level of trust we need to act together, I told him. We had to be able to work together in my classroom. He'd raised one eyebrow. "You're the one in charge."

'"We're going to be talking about Richard III," I now told the class. "And we won't just be talking about him, we'll be playing him too. And when I say 'playing' I don't mean 'pretending'. What I'd like us to do for the rest of the year is to *become* Richard III. That will take effort. I'm going to ask you get under his skin. What is he feeling? What is he thinking? Why does he do the things he does?"

'There was no change whatsoever in the students' faces. One girl blew a bubble with her gum.

'"Does anyone know what *Richard III* is about?" I asked.

'Silence. The bubble popped.

'"Does anybody know who Richard III was? Or Shakespeare?"

'I should have done a round of names at the beginning of the lesson, but the students had flustered me and now it was too late, I couldn't call on anyone by name to force an answer out of them. The only name everyone had heard was mine, spoken mockingly by that skinny boy.'

Hannah sighs. Down by the campfire someone starts singing. She stares ahead for a long time. I wait. When she started talking about her class I'd pressed my nails into my arm and hadn't let go, and now it was like someone else was holding me like that, the hand contorted and rigid and no longer in my control.

'Do you often speak to people who have secrets? As a psychiatrist, I mean.'

I laugh.

'Of course. I'm not sure people without secrets exist.'

'Big secrets I mean, which threaten to tip them over the edge.'

Almost all my patients have secrets like that, which they present to me as the reasons for their distress.

129

When you hear too many of those secrets it starts to get annoying, and the causal relationship becomes less plausible. Over the years I've come to believe that the distress was there first and the secret came along later, by way of an explanation.

'Do you have a secret like that, Hannah? Do you want to talk about it?'

She seems to hesitate, then shakes her head. Beating the grass off her clothes, she gets up. There's nothing I can say. I watch as she limps away, downhill, back to the others.

That night I can't sleep. Outside, the party refuses to die down while I lie inside, my arms across my chest, listening to the laughter and the strumming of guitars. The songs they're singing are oldies, music from another, more hopeful era and their voices too sound young and unscathed. Now and then the dull, sweetish smell of marijuana drifts into my room and once I hear Hannah declaiming, in an exaggerated, theatrical voice, 'I am a villain: yet I lie. I am not. Fool, of thyself speak well: fool, do not flatter.'

The sound of applause, laughter.

Shouts for an encore.

In the dark I listen to their voices, waiting as the cold envelops my body, waiting until I feel nothing.

The next morning only remnants are left.

The ashes, still glowing in the fire pit, our own dishes, covered in congealed fat, and a few goat bones that haven't been carried off by stray dogs.

'It was a good party,' I say to Hannah. We're outside, at the sink, trying to scrub bits of goat meat off the dishes. There are dark circles under her eyes. She hasn't looked at me all day.

'Yes,' she says. 'I want you to leave.'

It's so out of the blue that I don't know how to respond; for a moment I think I must have misheard. But she says it again: 'I want you to leave this place.'

'Why?'

'You've been here too long. You were never meant to stay on with me.'

At that moment, it's the afternoon already, Tina appears, yawning extensively. She greets us, before stumbling back into the house to make coffee.

'You can catch the train back to Sofia tomorrow. Or to Varna, although it's not exactly beach weather anymore.'

'I don't understand. Did I do something wrong?'

Hannah doesn't answer. Following the direction of her gaze, I see Tina coming towards us with steaming mugs. 'Ladies: coffee, tea!'

There's an awkward silence, but Tina doesn't seem to notice.

'How long will you be staying?' she asks, settling herself down on the grass.

I open my mouth and then shut it again, before looking at Hannah.

'She's looking for a new place,' she says.

'As a volunteer? Well, you're welcome to come to mine.'

So later that day I gather my things, roll up my sleeping bag and sweep the floor. I say an awkward goodbye to Hannah. We don't hug. I wonder if she only talked to me because she knew she was going to send me away. Or perhaps her openness has frightened her, and that's why she doesn't want to see me anymore. I don't have a say in the matter, I understand that now. So I squeeze myself into the small Lada next to Tina, and wave at Hannah as we drive off. The dog barks triumphantly.

Tina's house has more mod cons than Hannah's. She has a shower that isn't heated by a wood-burning stove, as well as an electric fire. There's not much to do. My main purpose is to be someone for her to talk to. I don't listen to what she says. Now and then I mumble something she takes for agreement. That's enough. Whole days pass in which nothing happens. I haven't spread out my things in Tina's spare room, I know I won't be staying here.

We're waiting, but I don't know what for.

She talks about her failed marriage, the man she stayed with for too long and who never appreciated her. All her stories are clichés.

Sometimes she asks me a question: why did I come here, do I like it? My answers are curt, just long enough not to seem rude. I can see Tina is already regretting her offer and is sulking because she isn't getting enough attention, I'm not the conversational partner she was hoping for. She won't be here for much longer, she's going back to her home country before the winter starts. 'I don't need to be here when it gets cold,' she giggles, drawing her shawl closer.

But the snow we've been expecting for a long while doesn't arrive.

It gets colder, but not much, and Tina stays on, for now. I don't know where I will go when she leaves.

We talk about Hannah a lot, because we don't have much else in common. Tina admires her, but pities her too. She's too hard on herself, Tina says. Why would you come here and make things so difficult for yourself, when luxury is so much cheaper here than at home? I shrug, pretending indifference, which only encourages her. Hannah is different to the others that have come to live here. She has no plan, no idea for a business that could secure her future. She never talks about herself, Tina says. 'It's as if she's cut all ties – makes you wonder why. I was so happy when I heard someone was coming to live in this village, a foreigner I mean, but it didn't turn out the way I thought it would. Still, she seemed friendly when I first spoke to her. But what can first impressions tell you about someone?'

She stops. This is the moment to ask her what she didn't see then, why Hannah isn't as friendly as she seemed at first. But I don't ask anything. Not doing what this woman expects of me gives me a perverse pleasure and, to my own surprise, I feel an urge to protect Hannah, though I'm not sure against what. I haven't forgotten why I came here. But I long for the silence we shared, the strangers we were together, with my son in between us.

When the news comes I'm not surprised. It's Tina who picks up the phone and then starts screaming. 'Oh God,' she says, 'oh my God.' She waves her plump little hand in front of her face in a typically American gesture. 'And I was just about to leave.'

While she talks she makes frantic gestures in my direction, so I stay where I am. Her cheeks are flushed now, her hair is messed up and her eyes shine. 'Oh God, how terrible. And who found her?'

Tina hangs up and collapses into an armchair, rubbing her brow like she's had a dizzy spell. For one awful moment I think Hannah is already dead, and I'll never know what happened to Kito. But still I ask nothing, just wait, staring at my feet.

'Aren't you going to ask me what happened?' Tina bursts out finally.

'What is it then?'

'They found her.' She draws out her words, cherishing her power. 'We need to get over there.'

I follow her to the car. She still hasn't told me what's happened, but I squeeze myself in next to her and try to look indifferent.

'She told you to leave, didn't she?' Tina asks as we turn onto the road leading to Hannah's house.

I shrug.

'It's nothing to be ashamed of, it happens to everyone. She likes you for a while and then, suddenly, it's all over. But she's going to need us now.'

I can hear the satisfaction in her voice. 'It's her own fault. If you'd still been around ...'

Hannah had hurt herself while chopping wood, the day after the party. She'd limped inside and had just lain there in the house, which grew cold after the *pechka*, the stove, went out, and she didn't have the strength to go out and get wood to fire it up again. She hadn't tried to warn anyone, not any of us or her Bulgarian neighbours, who found her by accident. They'd cleaned and dressed the wound on her leg, but they were worried about her and called Caroline who, in turn, called us. When Caroline asked the young man who called her what they were worried about, he remained vague. 'So it must be psychological,' Tina says, sounding gratified. 'The Bulgarians don't know how to deal with that kind of thing.'

We bump along the road to Hannah's house. As soon as Tina parks the car, the dog starts barking.

'So, here we go,' Tina says as we get out of the car. She looks at me for some sign of support I refuse to give.

Hannah's in her room, in bed.

She doesn't answer when we call her and turns her head away when we come in. We talk to her, our voices soft and reassuring, as if she's a child or someone who can't be trusted. She doesn't respond. I'm not sure she recognizes me. Strands of hair are stuck to her face and sweat glistens on her forehead, even though the house is cold. I get some wood from outside and put it in the *pechka*, blowing on the fire carefully to get it going.

Later that night she is delirious.

I'm sitting by the bed, while Tina circles around us, her phone permanently clamped to her ear. I ask her to get water and blankets and firewood. She listens to me and walks back and forth, sighing and complaining of tiredness, but with new-found respect for me in her eyes. The sky outside is the colour of lead, snow has been predicted.

'Do you mind,' Tina asks, 'if I get my ticket tomorrow? You look like you can manage here.'

The next morning she goes to the library, which has a computer with internet access, and books a flight for that same week. She needs to go back to her own house to get it ready for winter; she'll catch the bus to Sofia from there. 'There's Hannah's car, there's firewood, enough to last the winter. There's the neighbours, and you can always call Caroline.'

She honks the horn as she drives off, relieved. I wave and then walk back to the house, waiting a moment before going in. The dog throws itself against the bars of its cage and I stand there a second, looking down at it. 'I'm back,' I say. 'Whether you like it or not.'

I pick up a forgotten pumpkin and kick off my shoes on the veranda. It feels almost like coming home. Inside Hannah is asleep, shivering despite the blankets piled on top of her.

'So, here I am,' I say, looking down on the defenceless body of the woman who killed my son. 'And I won't be leaving again.'

I see one of her eyelids tremble. I clench my fists, but she's just tossing and turning, and then she lies still again. Asleep, she seems vulnerable as a child.

III

WHEN KITO SAW snow for the first time he panicked, unable to understand where the world he knew had gone. He hated the cold autumn rains, and he screamed with fear the first time he touched ice. He was cold most of the time and would cry until you wrapped him in blankets. Pressed tightly against your chest, he would finally fall asleep. 'It's the yearning,' you said to Mark then, 'he's brought it with him. And with the cold here, can you imagine how he must miss the warmth on his skin.'

But here, now, it isn't really cold, not the way you expected. Because there's no wind, or because your body can no longer feel the cold like it did before he disappeared. Yesterday the first snow started to fall, finally, in large, slow flakes. It was morning and the sky was a very light grey. From the window you saw the field gradually disappear.

You take care of Hannah now, watching her from the chair you've put in her room, next to the bed. She sleeps a lot; she isn't getting worse, but she isn't getting better either. Her eyes look huge in her face. The neighbours have checked the supply of firewood but haven't been round since. The world outside consists of the white of the snow and the black of the night, which is endless. The cold pulls people into their houses.

You fill the day with getting firewood, building up the fire, waiting, and then getting more logs. Feeding the dog. You help Hannah, dabbing her face and helping her onto the chamber pot, looking away when you empty it outside. She's ashamed of her body, but you tell her she shouldn't worry.

'I'm a mother,' you say. 'I've seen it all before.'

But you never quite felt at ease changing Kito's nappy, and in that sense it was a relief to have a child that didn't come out of your body and didn't suckle on your breasts – maybe it could never have been any other way.

'Tell me about your son,' Hannah says, because the silences are long and oppressive.

So you talk, looking for moments fit to display to her. The way he held a leaf up to his nose in autumn, smelling it ostentatiously like it was a beautiful flower; the little plays he would sometimes put on. And the way, later that afternoon, he ran after the blue balloon he'd been given with an ice cream. You watched him from a distance, his silhouette with one arm stretched out towards the balloon and Mark's tall shape behind him, and you felt this was everything, this was enough and it would stay this way. You talk about the drawings he made, the period he only drew birds, for months on end, after that one time, at the zoo, when a peregrine falcon landed on his shoulder. He hadn't dared breathe and had just looked, wide-eyed, at the animal's soft feathers and its hard, merciless beak. That seems to move her and she says, 'I once knew …' But then she's silent again and you don't press her, not yet.

You give her all those stories, everything that is nice and presentable, but you never say his name. She listens and says nothing, it's like she doesn't quite believe you and is still waiting for something, a missing part of the story. When she falls asleep you carry on talking and you find yourself saying he always remained an outsider, he never managed to become like the others, not on the inside. 'You can't understand what that does to a mother, to see that your child is the only one who doesn't belong, who's never really accepted.'

Children notice these things more quickly, they feel it.

When Kito had just started school he'd tried to make friends with another boy who was also new to the class, who was whacking the sand aimlessly with a spade. The boy had red hair, not strawberry blond or auburn but a shade of orange so bright you knew he was going to be picked on. You watched them from the stone edge of the sandpit, seeing Kito walk towards him carefully, holding out his bucket with sand. You wanted him to choose another child to be friends with, someone who fitted into the group more easily, like the girl over there or the boy in dungarees. Kito didn't see them. He just kept looking at that one little boy, who stood there, staring at him, before knocking the bucket out of Kito's hands and running away. In the boy's eyes you could see everything you'd just been thinking about him, the fear of being seen with someone who was almost certainly going to remain an outsider. Kito watched the boy run off. Then he picked up the bucket and carried on playing, alone.

What you hadn't expected was that he'd be so vulnerable you wouldn't be able to protect him. And nothing you tried, later, would make a difference, not designer clothes or resilience courses, because kids see straight through all that.

Hannah nods when you say that, suddenly alert. 'Some kids are like that. As a teacher you see it in their eyes, hear it in their voice. The art is to discover those children among the rest, who are mostly ugly, loud and crude. Because they don't even know it themselves and do their best to disappear. To discover them and draw them out is the best thing you can do as a teacher, it's the heart and soul of the job, I'd say.'

Suddenly she's an expert, but just look at her lying there with her leg, already weak and now messily bandaged, under that pile of old blankets. She could be a vagrant, she's lost everything.

'Did you do it on purpose?' I ask, suddenly. 'Hurting yourself, not asking for help?'

Because she showed you, when you'd just arrived, how to stand when chopping wood, so the axe wouldn't slip. She demonstrated it, her hands calloused and experienced, the swing powerful but controlled. You tried it yourself and only then did you appreciate the skill she'd demonstrated, realizing it must have cost time to acquire that suppleness.

She says, 'Sometimes you think a sacrifice is required, a penance. But, in the end, does anyone even care, is anyone bothered about your sacrifice?'

And then, again, 'Talk to me, tell me about your son.'

Hannah is too weak to go outside and you don't last long yourself at minus fifteen, even though there's no wind and it doesn't seem cold. The house is too small for two people. You've filled all the cracks and holes as much as possible to prevent the warm air from leaking out, but now there's hardly any ventilation. The smoke irritates your eyes and throat and the lack of oxygen gives you a headache. Everywhere you hear the sound of her breathing, moving around, swearing when she's in pain. Outside there's the endless, lead-coloured sky, which also weighs down on you. Hannah is peevish and unreasonable, her moods are fickle. You cook her food, but she pushes her plate away with disgust, without taking a bite. You don't know why you're making such an effort, but you are: you ask her what she wants to eat, you plump her cushions while she makes critical comments in a shrill voice, you don't get angry. It's a perverse pleasure caring for her like this, to keep smiling, not reacting when she lashes out at you, or later, when she cries and tells you she's sorry.

The work of the summer has given you back your body, the perimeter of your skin. Something that was gone for a long time has returned, an agility you had lost. For a long time it took a conscious effort to lift your arms, your legs, but somewhere along the way that changed, and now your body functions without you having to think about it. Undeniably, you are doing better than before. Sometimes you notice this, and you're surprised.

Ashamed.

Where will your child be if you don't carry him around? Who will think about him, who will keep him alive? So now your blood's started circulating again, you try to get back to that earlier state, the cold, desolate plain his death made of you. It's the only way you can

143

take care of him now, to cherish your hatred and not forget for a single moment why you came here. It's treachery to live only for yourself, but something inside you is carrying on, without you wanting it to.

Hannah feels that something's going on, there's a reason you're staying, but she doesn't know it has anything to do with her. She'd prefer to be alone, to walk out into the cold never to return, sinking slowly, but you won't allow it. They say it's a peaceful way to die, freezing to death, curling up in the snow and waiting. So you keep her alive, taking good care of her. Brushing the sweat out of her hair, wiping her forehead with a flannel. She doesn't trust you. Her eyes follow you around the room, but she says nothing. The snow muffles all sound, covers everything up. You talk to each other quite amicably.

You wait.

During these days you both know you are waiting, though you don't know for what, and while you wait the two of you talk about your child. Slowly, struggling to put one word after the other, you bring your dead son back to life, restoring him to the world. Using words, you sketch the way he moved, his eyes and the light inside them, the soft colour of his skin. You'd never realized how long, how unending his death would be. Never before have you been his mother as much as you are now, when he is no longer here, and you are blowing life back into his lost body. You have never been so close.

Once, while she's sleeping, you tell her, that she killed your son, she knew him, was the last to see him. She

144

moves restlessly and you stop, afraid she'll wake up, or already has. But her eyes remain shut and so you carry on talking, relieved you can finally say these things out loud.

'I don't feel guilty,' you whisper to her sleeping face. 'Whatever they may think, it wasn't my fault.'

'I miss the dog,' Hannah says when she wakes up. 'She has enough blankets, right? She's warm enough?'

'I think so. Should I bring her in?'

Not that sharing the already crowded space with a dog appeals to you, but Hannah's moods are unpredictable and it's important to humour her.

'She can't come inside. All the locals would laugh at me.'

'Who would even notice?'

'They'd think I was crazy.'

Sounding like she's thought about it a long time, later that same day she asks, 'As a psychiatrist you've been trained to understand why people do the things they do, even if they don't know themselves, right? That's what you've been trained to do?'

'We listen. We can administer tests, make diagnoses. The question is what they tell us.'

'They tell you whether someone's normal, right?'

'They give you a score.'

It's a long time before Hannah starts talking about herself again, but eventually it's like she takes a decision. Maybe it's because you're a psychiatrist; she expects something of you – a solution, a judgement, or just someone who'll listen. She wants to purge herself or prove she was right, maybe she truly believes talking will help expel the memories from her body. Perhaps she'd tell the story to any random stranger. But of course no one else would stay with her, no one without an ulterior motive, she should realize that.

People ascribe an authority to psychiatrists that we don't really possess. They think you can read their thoughts, deduce their secrets from little things like the way they drink their coffee or when they laugh. You can tell from the questions they ask you at birthday parties, the way they look at you. You know colleagues who keep their profession a secret for that very reason; one person you knew always introduced herself as a florist when meeting people she didn't know. ('What do you say if they ask you about flowers?' 'That I only ever use blue ones.'). It's that magic, or the false appearance of magic, that seems to be attracting Hannah now. You almost feel sorry for her because she's allowing herself to be fooled so easily, so keen to believe in a redemption you haven't even promised her.

'Sometimes something happens and you don't even realize it's happening and then you look back and wonder how it could have come to that, how things could have gone so wrong.'

'I'm listening.'

'There was a boy who disappeared, he was in my class.'

You stare past her at the door, counting the planks to keep your face expressionless. Silence is the best strategy to encourage patients to keep talking. If you refrain from answering for long enough, the other will nearly always try to fill the silence, reacting to the question you didn't ask. Usually they start with a denial, like you've made an insinuation they're now setting right. That thought has its roots in something: depending on the school you ascribe to, it is the voice of the significant other, the critical parent or maybe just their conscience – in any case, it's the voice that keeps them awake at night.

'It's not that I feel guilty,' Hannah says. 'There's nothing I could do about it, I know that. But I just can't get it out of my head.'

'Tell me about it,' you say, and your voice sounds very calm. 'Tell me what happened.'

You fold your hands under your chin and wait; it's important now to conform to her mental image of a psychiatrist.

'Teaching a bunch of kids that age,' she says, 'a class like that, which collects the heads of failed teachers as trophies, and teaching them drama too, not a straightforward, more clearly defined subject like maths or French – that's like being strapped to a bomb, I see that now. I didn't know it at the time, I was too young, and had such hopes. Maybe it was the films I watched, the books I'd read, it was all very well intentioned. I thought I had it in me to change them. I wasn't a great actress, never had been. But I did remember what acting had given me, even if I didn't feel it anymore, not the way I had when I was still at school myself. I was in the school play. Not the main part – I was the youngest sister and not important to the story but it was still a turning point, to feel someone else's words in my mouth, to repeat and repeat them until I made them mine, and I became someone else. Maybe it wasn't even acting itself that drew me in, but something the actors shared with each other but not with the audience: the camaraderie when they took a bow, the laughter as they disappeared off stage.

'Before that, there had always been my leg, the kind of thing your parents say doesn't matter but actually makes all the difference. My bad leg, as my mother called it. When I was a child I thought she meant it literally and when I'd been told off or wasn't happy about myself I'd hit it, the leg that didn't really belong to me, not like my other, healthy one. My handicap made me lonely and distrustful and though I was never really bullied I was never part of the group either. People don't like to see someone limping. Imperfection makes them uneasy, like a birthmark marring the face of a woman who would otherwise have been beautiful. My parents, too, were constantly reminded of my vulnerability; what gave them away were tiny gestures, movements, sentences left unsaid or unfinished. It was impossible to accept their love without experiencing a sense of humiliation at the same time.

'I was always aware of the discomfort I caused people around me, but there in the auditorium, with everybody watching, for the first time my fear of being laughed at had disappeared completely. I tried to stretch my lines out as much as possible, feeling the eyes of the audience on me, not watching me with pity, but fascination.

'It was because of that dizzying feeling I went to drama school, where my freedom didn't last long under the critical gaze of the teaching staff and their harsh words. Some of my classmates could take it – some of them really belonged on stage, and always had done. But I never really believed in it myself and that alone meant I wasn't going to make it, maybe at school but not outside, where all those classmates would be trampling all over each other for those few places in the spotlight.

'It was on the school's advice I went into teaching. A convenient recommendation from their point of view – one less to worry about – because of course teaching doesn't really count, not for those people. That was my greatest disappointment, that I'd learned to see myself through their eyes, judge myself through their eyes. No wonder my ambitions were too high when I started as a teacher; what else could I do?

'I made the wrong impression without realizing it, too naïve maybe for those students with their raging hormones, the blood beating in their bodies like a drum. They had reputations to keep, their honour to uphold, and there was everything they had yet to become, things they didn't even know themselves, the future and how important they were, how different to their parents, how normal.'

She stops, taking a breath and a sip of water. You watch her swallow, then take the glass from her, refill it and put it down beside her. She says, 'It's very strange to be able to speak my own language. Strange, to be talking to someone.'

It's like you've only just arrived here, the way she's looking at you, surprised almost.

'On the day of the second lesson it was raining heavily. By the time I'd got to school the dress I was wearing was soaked, its fabric plastered to my body. I was late, that second time; I'd been dreading leaving the house,

149

having to stand in front of that class, and I'd been putting the moment off for as long as possible. There was no time to dry off, so I rushed into the classroom with my soaking wet dress and dripping hair, panting from the bicycle ride. They were already in the classroom when I came in, standing around in groups, their arms crossed nonchalantly. This is what I'd been dreading all night, their eyes ...'

Up till now she's been talking to the ceiling, but now she suddenly looks you directly in the eyes, almost reproachfully.

'Do you have any idea what that feels like, to stand there while they stare at you, to keep talking even though you know you've already lost, they're not interested. The things that fascinate you, the knowledge you have, the person you are: all of this you give to them. And there you stand, talking to the air. You hear your own voice and things aren't going well. They look away, they look at each other, they laugh about something, possibly you. You stand there, and the only thing you have is your body, vulnerable and unprotected.

'Some people wear dark-blue clothes on days like those, or wrap a band of tinfoil around their waist.' She laughs uneasily. 'It's a little weird, but it does help. They do it to protect their bellies, it's a kind of magic. Though exposing oneself like that was something I would be asking of them, too, those kids whose names I didn't know yet. But when I came in, that second lesson, and didn't know what to expect – in the preceding days I'd grown increasingly desperate while I sat at home alone at night and watched darkness fall, the series of lessons seemingly destined to be a failure already – when I came in, that tall, thin boy, the one who wouldn't take his cap off in the first lesson, he took a step forward, took his cap off with a sweeping movement and made a bow.

'It was a strange gesture, courteous and old-fashioned, and it was so out of place I didn't know what was happening. But I reacted without thinking, bowing to him in turn. When I straightened up I saw he was smiling. He had beautiful, steel-blue eyes and long, dark eyelashes. I could hear whistling and someone started clapping. The class was confused, rudderless. The boy's name was Timothy. Apart from being the tallest, he was also older than the rest of the class.

'They looked at him.

'They tried to read his facial expression so they could follow him, do the right thing. His reaction, so different to what they'd expected, had left them helpless.

'It was only later on I heard more about him in the staffroom. There was trouble at home: his father unemployed, a difficult relationship. Social services had been involved; he was at-risk, vulnerable. But in that class he was the absolute ruler. He had the power to destroy me, and he chose not to, at least not yet.

'He took a bow.

'He bowed towards me and I said, to the whole class, "Let's start again."

'I really believed that was possible then.

'We started the lesson with trust building exercises – allowing yourself to fall into someone else's arms, that kind of thing. I let them choose their own partners, and predictably enough this meant the class reject was left on his own. He was the only black kid in the class. He wore straight-legged corduroy trousers, a shirt

151

and a pullover. His voice was too high and his serious expression also marked him out; it contrasted with the affected indifference the others worked so hard at. Finally, there was the leather bag he carried with him, the kind only older teachers have and kids like him, who you can tell are going to be picked on from the start. He was called Kito, and it didn't suit him; a name like Charles, Tarquin or Ernest would have been better.'

You listen to her, you don't move a muscle. You want to go outside, but you're scared she won't carry on talking if you do. At the same time you want to stop her. She's still weak and it wouldn't take much to silence her forever. Silence her: maybe that's the word, the perfect synonym you were looking for. You could force her to keep her story, her judgements and her stupid comments to herself. What did she know about him and what suited him? Still, this is the woman he wrote his last letter to, if it deserves that name. Or maybe it was someone imitating his handwriting, but even if that was the case you still need to know, you need to find out why he trusted her.

Hannah is oblivious to what you're thinking. She doesn't even need you, she just keeps talking.
'I walked up to him and stood there.
'"Let yourself fall," I said, "and I will catch you."
'He stared at me.
'"Go on."
'He just stood there.
'I insisted and then he suggested turning it around, so he'd be the one catching me. Of course I refused; he

152

was so much smaller than me, my weight would be too much for him.

'"See," he said, "you don't trust me either."

'I didn't know what to say to that and so I turned to the other students, who found the exercise hilarious. He stood at the window with his arms behind his back, like a little old man. He was the only one who refused to take part, just standing there, his straight back like a reproach.

'At the end of the lesson I once again asked the question Richard asks himself in the end, desperate and close to death: "Is there a murderer here?"

'I looked around the classroom, searching, looking each of the students in the eye. Timothy stared straight back. Kito looked at the floor. A few of the girls giggled. "No. Yes, I am."

'The class waited. For the first time, I had their attention, and I had to seize the moment.

'"Imagine having to ask yourself that question. And having to answer 'Yes, I am.' This Richard has done terrible things. He's a hunchback, he's ugly and he's always been an outsider. He's taken his revenge, he's murdered people in the hope of being accepted, of coming out on top. But now he's on his own. He's alone and afraid of the dark, afraid of the morning that's coming, afraid of dying. Afraid of the very people he's murdered. I want you to imagine what that's like, to put yourself in his place. And that means breathing the way he breathes and sweating the way he does," – more giggles at this point, and cries of "that's so gross" – "sharing his dreams and his fears, making his words your own. Starting from next week, you will all be called Richard."

'When they left that day they sounded different: they were loud as usual, but there was an underlying note of expectation. As they walked away I heard them shout to each other "Hey, Richard!", "Richard", their voices echoing in the hallway. The tone was mocking but not scornful – playful perhaps. That was good enough for me, I was happy.'

It's a while before you notice Hannah's stopped talking. The room is cold and it's gone dark already. You get up to get more logs from outside. Hannah's words hang suspended in the room and it's a relief to open the door and step out into the snow and the cold evening air.

You push snow against your skin until it burns and then you cram it into your mouth until it feels like you're choking. Then you get a jar of preserved gherkins from the basement, making sure your face is smooth, unruffled, before you go back inside with the jar and the logs. You build up the fire and make dinner. It's good to have something to do, to move about and have a purpose. Hannah won't eat anything. She stares at the ceiling and doesn't answer when you say goodnight.

Once in bed you can't get it out of your head how, apparently, he stood there on his own in front of the window, how alone he was. To dispel the image you picture setting fire to the vine next to the house. You see how the first flames will lick the house quite gently and carefully, until it is too late and the fire becomes furious and uncontrollable. You see it all disappear, this house and all your empty words, until the only thing left is an open space, the ashes of what used to be.

154

But the next morning you make breakfast for her again: fried eggs and bacon, a hearty breakfast.

'You need to eat properly.' You sound cheerful, like you're going on an outing.

She sniffs the greasy air and mumbles something you can't make out. You don't ask her to repeat it. You wander aimlessly around the room, which is too small, straightening a chair, wiping away some dust. You go outside and feed the dog, who growls at you.

Hannah sniffs as you come back inside.

'It's ironic, travelling all this way, making this place for myself, working the land, painting the walls, the woodwork – that green paint is poisonous you know, it's from the communist era – and it still hasn't made me happy.'

'Happiness is an awfully big word.'

'But it's what we're looking for.'

You don't like talk about happiness, because it presumes there once was such a thing as a golden age of pure, lasting joy. You don't believe in things like that, it's a question of discipline.

'How difficult can it be, actually, happiness, is it really so much to ask?'

She sounds aggrieved; you say nothing. When you'd just started as a psychiatrist you'd asked a patient if she believed the happiness she was looking for so desperately really existed. The woman had stared at you, distraught. She stopped her treatment shortly after.

Hannah pushes her plate away, saying, 'That week was the best one. I didn't know that at the time. The way they listened to me during that second lesson, that was something I hadn't experienced very often. It seemed a near miracle after that disastrous start.

'After that first lesson I was afraid to look Maureen in the eye. I didn't pick up the phone when she called me.

'Although we worked on different days, one way or another she was going to find out, that's the way it works in a school. And then she'd ask me, carefully, if I'd thought of something else I wanted to do with my life. But after that second lesson I called her myself to ask her if she wanted to meet up. I could hear her concern over the phone, even though she didn't put it into words. But when we were sitting in our usual cafe that evening, a bottle of wine on the table between us, she said how well I was looking. It was true, I could feel it myself.

'That one lesson awoke something in me I hadn't been sure was there anymore. It was the desire to get through to those kids, to go straight through their skin, peeling back all those layers to uncover something beautiful and tender that trembled – so I was convinced – deep down inside them.

'Kids that age are dangerous but special; they haven't learned to close themselves off like we have. They're not numb yet, but receptive, they really see things. Their parents, teachers, all of us – we ascribe everything they do and feel to puberty, and that's that. But no one feels as intensely as kids of that age, with all their desires and dreams. Quite suddenly, they see very clearly who we are, all those people they've always looked up to. They see how small we've become and how disappointed we are, and they don't give in to it. Resistance is still possible at that age, and you really think it will make a difference.

'That's the kind of thing I said to Maureen that night.

'She traced the edge of her wineglass with one finger.

'"It's what they want themselves, to be unmasked," I said. "They want to be exposed, even though they don't realize it. They're longing for something they can't put into words."

'Maureen told me to be careful. She tapped me on the hand but didn't look me in the eye.

'"What do I need to be careful about?"

'But I knew what she meant, even though she didn't say it. She'd always looked out for me. Compared to Maureen, my feelings were always too intense and uncontrollable, and I'd always stumbled from one situation into another, while she followed me, providing sensible advice. Some friendships are like that. We didn't talk about school again that night. We talked about her life; unlike mine, it had a solid shape to it, with a boyfriend and a cat.

'She wanted to get married, she said. They were thinking about having a baby.

'As long as thinking is all you're doing, I joked, but she didn't think that was funny. When we hugged each other later I felt how cold her fingers were. I was disappointed. Maureen had been living with her boyfriend for a long time and I liked going to their place, sitting on their sofa with my knees drawn up while I watched them make dinner. Then, after we'd eaten I'd do the dishes and it was as if we were still room-mates, like when we were students. I knew I didn't belong with them, and I'd have to walk back to my own house, alone, but I tried my best to forget that. I assume they saw me as a kind of project, and he tolerated me because she'd known me so long.

'I tried not to think about it.

'I'd been friends with Maureen since primary school, maybe that's why I couldn't imagine things would ever change. But there you had it: marriage, a child – their life would become closed off. In the months before I'd been to a number of friends' and acquaintances' weddings. Each time I watched the married couple, I was ashamed of the envy I felt. While the other people danced and the party carried on around me, I sat on the side. When people asked me something I used my leg as an excuse, but I had to do my best not to cry, not to give in to the melancholy feeling that seemed to get worse as the music grew more cheerful.

'Of course there were things I could have tried. I could have found a hobby or signed up to a dating site. But somehow it seemed too late for that and I didn't like the idea of having to tell some stranger about my leg. I couldn't think what the right moment would be, how to choose between my fear of either putting him off prematurely or disappointing him when, unprepared, he saw me in the flesh.

'So I just waited. My life was something that hadn't started yet. I was waiting for the right moment, a sign, because that was what I was like then; I always needed someone else to call me. In some strange way I didn't quite understand, all this was related to my leg. I was ashamed of it, the lack of symmetry, and so I'd taught myself to stay in the background. In another time or another country I would have become something radical, a terrorist. I would have looked for a purpose large enough to fill my body, a direction I could cling to.

'Now I trudged home and when I got there I had to force myself to go inside, where it was cold and dark and no one was waiting for me. I switched on the lights and turned up the heating, but the light was too bright and hurt my eyes. I imagined everything would stay the same. I'd slowly grow old here, and every now and then I'd go and visit Maureen and her kid who would never grow to like me because I was too desperate for its attention. The things I'd said earlier that night now seemed empty and pretentious and I was angry at myself because I'd let myself go, but especially because I'd told Maureen something I should have kept to myself, something she couldn't understand.

'That night I couldn't bear to stay in the house, I had to get out. I put my coat back on and cycled to the dunes, even though it had long since gone dark and it was cold for the time of year. There's something magical about walking through an area like that on your own in the dark, with the stars above you and now and then the shrill cry of a seagull, and nothing else around but silence, which takes on a presence of its own. I took the path leading through the dunes to the beach. Even though I knew it well, I found the shifting sand hard going, and the short walk to the sea more tiring than I expected. More than once I was on the point of turning back, driven by that primeval fear of the dark everyone has experienced as a child. But I carried on walking. I couldn't suppress a feeling of triumph when I reached the final dune and looked out at the sea, waiting for me, black and seemingly endless. It was only when my leg responded to my euphoria with increasingly intense shooting pains that I realized how tired I was and how

I'd have to cover the whole distance again on the way back. I pushed that thought away though, staring out at the lights in the distance, the ships lying off the coast like mechanical whales.

'As I was standing there with my bare feet in the water, something happened to me which is difficult to describe. It was a moment of well, grace – I can't think of a better word – a deep realization that everything was good, everything was all right the way it was. At that point I didn't feel the cold anymore, there was just the water, black and endless, and the barely distinguishable sky. Later I only barely managed to get back, stumbling home, and I was hardly able to move my leg for days afterwards. But I'd been given something that was more important than a few days of pain.

'Looking back, it's easy to explain away that feeling: the effects of alcohol, exhaustion, a trick of the brain. But it was more than that. There on the beach it dawned on me that maybe my excessive emotions weren't just an inconvenience, but were, on the contrary, a kind of sixth sense, a sensitivity most people lacked.'

You snort when she says that, you can't help it.

Hannah looks up like she's only just remembered you're there. 'I know you're not supposed to say things like that about yourself. But it was true and later they felt it too, the kids, or at least some of them. The same thing that had made me so vulnerable during the first lesson helped me get closer to them later, because I was genuinely interested in all those feelings they were afraid to admit to themselves, even when they were alone.'

In the evening you try to put down her words on paper, exactly as she said them, but it takes an effort to write them down. All those thoughts and explanations, the justifications before she's even confessed anything. This is also a possibility: that she'll tell you everything and you'll still be none the wiser at the end of her story. She has buried the truth under thick layers of words; what really happened is hidden deep inside her.

You'd have to claw your way in, through her skin.

You'd have to push your way through to get past her story, the empty sentences she's pouring all over you. You imagine how she must have sat there after that first lesson, alone in her tastelessly decorated flat. She'd never planned to become a teacher, but it had happened anyway – not good enough for the real stage, not the right type of person, she didn't know the right people or didn't want to sleep with them, and now here she was, standing in front of a bunch of teenagers who didn't like her and despised the subject she taught. She was probably bullied herself, being the one who would, in the animal world, be bitten to death or pecked until she was bare and bleeding. And yet she had hopes, that first day, even though she should have known better, and that same night she tried to think of how, in the next lesson, she could undo her mistakes, restoring the balance. She has a disability but she's not ugly. She's old enough to suggest some experience, but young enough to be free of visible signs of decay. Is it any wonder the boys in the class are restless and Timothy welcomes her with a bow, the attention he pays her now contrasting sharply with his earlier indifference and contempt?

She's flattered, she believes that people are essentially good.

The leader bows, and the class hesitates. The boys start clapping while the girls lean back and look her up and down, their expressions vacillating between contempt and distrust. They look at each other and at Timothy, who pretends not to see them looking, cultivating his whims like any other absolute ruler. Because that was what he had, absolute power, that was clear to you even from a distance. You saw it from the edge of the playground, watching his followers gather round him, doing their best to get his attention. It was only when he was at your house, on his own, that he'd seemed small and unsure of himself and gradually that image had pushed aside the rest, so that in the end you thought of him mostly as that lanky kid. That's what you wanted to believe, that maybe he was Kito's friend, his only friend. That was how you created a friend for him, even if it was only one. As long as he hadn't died alone, as long as you could tell yourself that, as long as someone had been with him.

Later you ask her about Timothy.

'What kind of boy was he?' you ask, and she perks up – she seems fascinated by him, even now, after all this time.

'He wasn't ugly like Richard III, but of all his classmates he was the one best suited to the role. He had the same air of grievance, and the ruthlessness that can produce, convinced that he had a right to be compensated. I don't believe in evil, but that boy had something in him, something essential that had become twisted a long time ago, maybe even before he was born. He was the type you imagine torturing animals, secretly kicking a cat to death. But everyone still did their best to get him to notice them, they all wanted to exist in his eyes. The girls moved differently when they were around him, and the boys were just a little bit louder and less sure of themselves.

'My class functioned only when he allowed it to – if Timothy was having a bad day, there would be nothing doing. They wouldn't listen to me, turning their backs to talk among themselves, and leaving the classroom just half an hour into the lesson.

'On those days Kito was the only one who stayed behind, obediently, alone with me in the otherwise empty classroom. He had no talent for acting: fear was the only emotion he could perform convincingly. I don't know if he felt anything else. Without conviction he spoke the words "Is there a murderer here?"

'I encouraged him to look for the source of creativity that had to be hidden deep inside him. But he kept himself tightly under control, banning all spontaneity. He only stayed because he was supposed to and because he didn't want to go home, didn't want to cross the playground, past the group that always hung around the bike shed smoking.

'They played jokes on him: the dogshit in his bag, the drawings in his textbook he was afraid to look at, the coat that suddenly disappeared and was never seen again.

'He never complained.

'He was nervous and bit his nails to the quick. Now and then a tic contorted his face. That happened more

163

often when the others were around. When they had a mind to, they pelted him with apple cores or cans or whatever they had at hand. When I saw them do it I told them to stop, but then they weren't allowed to eat or drink in class either. Neither were they allowed to wear hats or coats or speak in their own language. All things I could no longer forbid them from doing in my classroom because I had failed to do so in the first lesson. So instead my classroom became a free state, a space where the rules didn't count, and like in any free state, survival of the fittest was the norm.

'Just once, another teacher stopped by my class. Her name was Astrid and she taught English. I'd invited her to give a guest lesson in the vague hope of making contact with the other teachers, who said hello in the hallways but never stopped for a chat. I heard their conversations in the staffroom, I knew everything about them. Sometimes I asked them about their kids, their spouses or the new kitchen, and they'd look surprised. They would answer me but I was left feeling I'd eavesdropped on a conversation that wasn't meant for my ears. They never asked me anything in return.

'But Astrid loved Shakespeare, encouraging her students to visit the Globe during the annual trip to London. I invited her to fill us in on the historical context, even though I wasn't interested in that aspect of the play. If it was up to me I'd cut the bewildering number of characters, just skip over the historical plot altogether.

'Astrid gave a point-by-point lecture about Shakespeare. She mentioned the mysteries surrounding his authorship and the important role cross-dressing plays in his work. The students seemed relieved to be taught in the traditional way, which allowed them to sit there safely with their exercise books before them. They'd also taken their hats and coats off at the start of the lesson, without Astrid having to say a word. She talked about how, in those days, boys would play the female roles, but that these characters in turn would take on another guise: boys pretending to be women pretending to be men.

'That made them laugh.

'Timothy said, "Sounds like something the poof should try," provoking shrill whistles. There was only one person he could have been referring to, and everyone looked at him. He pretended not to notice, staring at the caps of his neatly polished shoes while the whistling around him built up to a storm.

'Astrid looked at me briefly, waiting for me to intervene. When she realized I wasn't going to, that I was scared to, she calmly folded her reading glasses and looked at the class seriously. Just like that, they fell silent. It was almost like they were ashamed of having let themselves go.

'"Shakespeare," Astrid said – and I almost expected her to raise a finger in the air – "Shakespeare was the first person to portray the ambiguity of the human psyche in a convincing way."

'Uncomprehending faces.

'"How we want one thing, but we want the opposite at the same time. How our minds are dragged this way, and then that. How we're never just one person, but many different people in one body."

'From my spot at the back of the classroom I watched the impossible happen, how she genuinely taught these kids something, connecting abstract notions to their daily lives. But then this woman had been teaching her whole life; she stood upright like a soldier.

'After the lesson I walked beside her to the bicycle shed.

'"They really listen to you," I said. "How do you manage it? Do you have any magic tips for me?"

'She put her shabby old bag on the back of her bike and fixed it in place.

'"I think it's best someone tells you this very clearly," she said, wheeling her bicycle out of the shed before stopping to look me in the eye. "There aren't any tricks or tips or magic bullets. It's very simple really. You can teach: that's what I do. Or you can work in education, which is what you're doing."

'Then she cycled off on her old-fashioned bike, the long panels of her coat flapping in the wind. It wasn't until I went back to get my own bike that I saw Kito standing there, on the other side of the bike shed. He looked away immediately and so I pretended I hadn't seen him either. But each time I saw him after that, I was aware that he'd heard that conversation. It made me feel a vague aversion towards him, which I was ashamed of.

'Teachers have meetings about kids like that, in which we dissect the one who's being bullied, laying all their weak points out on the table one by one, among the mugs with the school logo, and then looking at them and shaking our heads. We recommend they do an assertiveness course, or take up a sport or a hobby, something that will make them stronger, build character. Now and then someone, usually the form teacher, has a serious talk with the class. Whether that happens and how depends on the parents and how much fuss they make. Because everybody knows it won't help. The relationships within the class have already been fixed and can't be changed, not by an outsider. When it comes down to it, teachers are always outsiders.

'When I was working at the school there had just been a few notorious cases of bullying that had got so out of hand they reached the papers. There had been calls to put a stop to this kind of thing once and for all. Maybe some people really believed that was possible – I didn't. I wasn't as cynical as the older teachers, but I knew what you could do and when there was no point even trying. But everyone needs a goal, something to aim for, even if it's an illusion. Something to get up for in the mornings. What can you do? You can hope they'll want to learn something from you, be prepared to take something of what you tell them on board. And you can hope maybe there will be one you really get through to, who will be changed in some real way and remember what you say for longer than a week. You hope you'll be able to give something, if only to one person – an image or a sentence, a feeling or a thought, something they didn't have before.

'Most of the time nothing changes.

'But you need to keep hoping something could happen if you tried hard enough. If you can't keep believing that, you won't be able to keep it up, either you'll fall apart in front of the class or you'll be gradually bled dry until one morning you notice there's nothing left of you. I hadn't reached that point at my previous schools, but I'd come close enough to know how terrifying it is.

'You say, "Sit down," and they don't listen.

167

'You say it again.

'And as you say it you hear your own voice, and how something is missing. Authority is what they call it, but actually it's the foundation under everything you say and what you do and how you stand. It's the foundation that's missing when you say it yet again and they still won't listen and you start to panic, your voice sounding more and more hollow, until even you no longer believe yourself.

'Teachers know what it's like to be bullied; we are dependent on the group's goodwill ourselves. But that doesn't mean we sympathise with the weakest. On the contrary, it's painful to watch kids like that who do everything wrong, calling down the wrath of the group. They cause trouble, these underdogs, forcing you to intervene. But that's risky, and so you look the other way. You pretend not to see how they bait him, snatching his things, passing notes with his name and some message that makes everyone laugh. Maybe he's asked for it in some way, and it's better to let them sort it out among themselves. And even if you did intervene, there are the long hours after school, and all the places teachers don't see – the bike shed, the bushes. Anything you try to do for him will be used against him, and so you do nothing.

'It's also because you realize how little you understand their world, their insecurities. They know they should be heading somewhere, but they don't know where. So much is expected of them and their dreams are still so big. They have opinions that aren't based on much but which they defend fanatically. Their bodies change, unrecognizably sometimes. What used to be familiar disappears and suddenly they observe things so sharply it hurts; they see straight through everything and it makes them sad. Sad to have found out how things really are, different to what they'd hoped. And suddenly they possess that magical capacity that makes them lonely and can't be shaken off, because they're too young to numb themselves effectively.

'I'd never been that kind of kid myself. But I was secretive, withdrawn, with an intensity that didn't show on the outside. When my parents fought I imagined myself dying and how sorry they'd be when they buried me, what they'd say. Then I'd feel ashamed of my thoughts, and my shame would be wild and uncontrollable. And then, shortly after, I'd think about what I would be, later, how beautiful I'd be; then again, I'd look in the mirror, convinced no one would ever love me, not with that leg, never. I was constantly hoping a teacher would notice me, would remember me much later on, but I never met anyone's gaze in the corridors. That's why I sympathized with their aimlessness.

'I was convinced theatre could change everything for kids that age. Sometimes the only way to be really honest is by playing someone else, and I've often thought the trouble with teaching is that you're standing there as yourself. You can try to pretend you're different, more interesting, but they see through that and usually punish you for it.

'Kito flinched when I asked him to stay behind after the lesson, avoiding my gaze for the rest of the hour. Even after the class had emptied he still didn't look at me; he just waited.

'I was irritated by his passive attitude and his slumped shoulders.

'"I want to help you, Kito."

'He said nothing.

'Through the classroom window I could see the faces of some of his classmates, trying to catch a glimpse. I waved at them to go away, but they stayed where they were, their noses pressed to the glass, giggling.

'"I have plenty of time," I said. My voice didn't even sound reassuring to myself.

'"What do you want me to do, Miss?"

'Unlike the other students, he'd always carried on addressing me with "Miss", and that also stung me, the distance he maintained so carefully.

'"I can help you."

'"It's not necessary, thank you."

'But he was too polite to leave without my permission. I took a step forward and I saw him tense his muscles. I reached out my hand to him and he just let his arms hang down. I took one of his hands and although he didn't try to stop me, I could feel him withdraw from that hand. I lifted his arm and made as if I wanted to dance with him. He just stood there. I let go of his arm.

'"You should let yourself go a little, Kito. You'll need that later on."

'He looked at me as if I was an unpredictable animal, measuring the distance between us, getting ready to flee at any second, but he didn't move.

'"Do I annoy you?" I asked. "You think I'm annoying, don't you? Say it. Just say that I'm annoying."

'He cleared his throat.

'"Just say it," I said. "Say how awful you think this is. How much you hate drama. It's true, isn't it?"

'He mumbled something I couldn't make out. He stared at me in total incomprehension, no doubt asking himself what he'd done to deserve this.

'"Louder. Say it. Shout it."

'More mumbled words.

'"Louder."

'He looked like he was about to cry and I wondered if what I was doing was wrong. I was thinking about stopping, when something moved in his face and it suddenly burst open.

'"I hate theatre!" he shouted. He withdrew back into himself the moment after, surprised by the sound of his own voice.

'"How do you feel about theatre?" I persisted, but he wasn't responding anymore.

'Only when I'd given up and was turning around to get my things did he shout it out again, so suddenly it made me jump. "I hate it, I hate it, I hate it!"

'It took a while before I noticed he was crying, in little, nervous jolts. That was also the moment I heard the laughter of the kids on the other side of the glass.

'I told him we'd stay behind again after the next lesson, that I wanted him to be able to really show his true self in my classroom, if nowhere else. I said, "You don't have to tell me, but at least write down what you really feel," and I gave him a pen and a piece of paper.

'He looked at me suspiciously. "Now?"

'"Now. There's no right or wrong moment to change your life."

'He hesitated, then wrote something down. Even his handwriting was small and it leaned forward, going right to the edge of the page.

'"Would you like me to know what you've written down?"

'Startled, he looked up. He'd just started folding the piece of paper into smaller and smaller squares. Now he handed it to me with visible reluctance, as if afraid to refuse. Unfolding it, I saw he'd only written one sentence: *I can't go on.*

'"It'll be all right," I said. "You have to believe me, things will get better."

'He sniffed loudly, then wiped the tears from his cheek with one hand, like they belonged to someone else. The kids outside had disappeared, but maybe they were waiting for him somewhere else, beyond the jurisdiction of the school. But still I went home knowing I'd achieved something; I'd given the boy a voice, or the beginning of one.

'Among themselves, the other students spoke a language I didn't completely understand. It was the speed at which they exchanged words and the effort they made to adopt another persona – streetwise, hard, damaged. I listened to them when they came into the classroom and sometimes I tried to imitate them, when I was at home and no one could hear me. Their language sounded awkward coming from my mouth. Later I made use of that, addressing them as bitches and bros, and they'd start to laugh in disbelief, with the kind of condescension reserved for foreigners who can't speak the language and are therefore funny and touching. They tried to teach me their words, the unarticulated

172

way you were supposed to spit them into the air. My attempts to copy them weren't successful and that made them laugh again, asking me to say something and then copying the way I copied them, how "well polite" it sounded, how pathetic. They recorded the sound, posted videos on YouTube. LOL, is what the comments said, LOL.

'But it wasn't meant unkindly, and when they laughed I laughed along with them, even louder than them. Sometimes I saw them outside school; they weren't as hyped up then and less on their guard. I was proud that they complained to me about the teachers who gave marks and had to work through set textbooks with them. Because I was young and just a substitute, I didn't have any real colleagues or sense of loyalty. When the students complained to me I was inclined to take their side and sometimes I did, even though I knew it was dangerous to say things like that aloud.

'They loved death. It attracted them, things that were dark and gory and too big to comprehend. They used cheap, nasty smelling deodorant and were always talking about sex, the boys crude and the girls giggling. Without exception they all wanted to be rich and famous, and they talked about the things they would have later, the labels they would wear. How they'd be like the people on TV. That was another way in, the dreams they had, and just for a moment even I believed in the promises I held out to them, the future ahead of them. But I sounded too enthusiastic and during the break I heard them say, "If she was any good she wouldn't be here, would she? Duh!" They wanted to study economics or law, degrees you could earn decent money with.

'I was someone who puzzled them. Because I'd chosen a subject they couldn't see the point of. Not wanting to correct them, to civilize them, made me different to their parents and the other adults, and therefore difficult to take seriously. I was an entertaining distraction. If nothing out of the ordinary had happened they would have forgotten me even before I'd found another job. Only there was that, what should I call it, that incident.'

'The disappearance.'

She hesitates. 'That's what I called it, yes. That's what you could call it.'

'What I don't understand,' she says, 'is how you can just sit there and listen to me. You always seem so calm, but it must do something to you, what I'm telling you —'

'My mind's divided into compartments,' I interrupt quickly. 'What you tell me goes into one of those compartments and then I close it, I turn the key.'

'Is that healthy?'

'Healthy is whatever allows you to function.'

But you're surprised yourself that you're able to do it. Making the quiet, understanding noises she expects, a paragon of empathy. Just sitting there, doing nothing, while her story brings you, irrevocably, to his death.

Later she returns to the conversation. 'Is that all there is? Just functioning I mean. We're not machines, are we?'

'What more would there be?'

She shrugs. 'I don't know. What about self-realization? Happiness?'

'They're just empty words, marketing; magazines are full of them.'

'How can you call happiness an empty word?'

174

She sounds genuinely hurt.

'I asked my son what he wanted to be once. "If you could choose anything, what would you really like to be?" "A bird," he answered. "A bird of paradise."'

Hannah turns around. 'I used to have a friend who would start her performance by asking the audience what animal they'd like to be. She stopped doing that pretty quickly; everyone, and I mean everyone, wanted to be a cat.'

'Why am I telling you all this?' she asks. 'What's the point, in the end?'

You cross one leg over the other and lean towards her. 'You sound disappointed. What's making you feel that?'

Your voice sounds measured, businesslike. She feels it too, that she can't hurt you, and she's protesting against her own powerlessness. It's a good thing the roles have been divided, that they're fixed. It gives you something to go by, a voice to assume and words to borrow.

'It's something you do,' she says. 'I don't know why, but I can feel how much you want to hear this. I'm not stupid, if that's what you're thinking.'

'I'm listening. I'm listening to what you say, but you can stop whenever you like.'

'You wouldn't stay here if I didn't have anything left to tell, would you? Are you listening as a psychiatrist, does it interest you? There are taxis you can take, the trains run in winter. You could go to Sofia and catch a plane.'

'I'll make us some tea.'

'Why don't you go home? What's left for you here, what do you want from me? Are you going to turn this into an article, a case that'll make you famous? I have nothing.' She holds her hands up, and starts to laugh.

You stand up and walk over to the stove. Then you change your mind and go outside.

'I have nothing left,' she calls after you. 'Nothing!'

On the veranda you clench your fists, and then stretch out your fingers again. Standing in the dark, you listen to her laughing.

After her outburst, you have to keep yourself from insisting she go on, doing your best not to show her in any way how you're waiting for the moment she'll pick up her story again. She watches you. You read. You leaf through *Bulgarian for Beginners* and stare at the same page for ages. 'How are you getting on with that?' she asks, scornfully.

It's not unusual for patients to project their feelings onto you. No therapy would be successful unless someone took on this symbolic role, temporarily donning the robe of the mother, the father, the absent other. These days you're supposed to leave that job to other, lesser-paid underlings, but you're familiar with the dynamic of attraction and rejection, of yearning – and then renewed resistance.

The problem, always, is how to put aside that role and become yourself again. To define the limits of what you are able to do, and make it clear to your patients that you can't prevent their fall, their destruction. What you can provide is routine, the time you have available, and a friendliness that is purely professional and means nothing. What they yearn for is real attention and the feeling that they're special. But you can't give them what they want and that makes them angry. They rattle at the bars of the conversation, kicking against the confines of your job description, and you look on, smiling, full of empathy, but that smile too is purely professional.

It's the attention they become addicted to; Hannah's no different in that sense.

She says, 'The thing that scares me is what if this doesn't work out, what can I do then? What can I do with my life?'

You're sitting behind her on the couch, brushing her hair. She could do it herself, but these kinds of rituals developed when she was really ill; it's hard to let go of them now. It's good if she becomes dependent on you and increasingly vulnerable, or that's what you tell yourself. In reality you yearn for the warmth of another body, it's been so long since you felt anything.

'Why shouldn't it work out?' you ask and she shrugs, then cowers down when you tug on a tangle.

Both of you are dirty under your thick layers of clothing. Now and then you heat water for the shower, but firewood is expensive and Hannah urges you to use it sparingly. 'We need enough to keep the *pechka* burning all winter.'

That means a shower is a luxury. There are days when you smell the sour odour of your own body. It's sick, the thing you desire; it's something you'd like to scrub out of your skin, but water won't help with that.

'Why shouldn't it work out?'

She waves her hand in the direction of the world outside the window. 'You think all this will stay this way by itself. But for years and years thistles and nettles grew here, the soil is full of their seeds. If you want to

177

grow anything here you need to pull out the weeds and burn them, and you need to do the same the next year and the year after that. You can't let up for a moment. We've made nature into something vulnerable and pitiable, but it isn't. It's merciless and mean; you can't turn your back on it for a moment.'

Later you go for a walk and when you get back Hannah is sitting at the table with a bottle of *rakia* in front of her. She watches you stamp the snow from her boots on the veranda, and take off her coat – you weren't prepared for the cold, you hadn't thought you'd be staying so long you'd need winter clothes.

'It's beautiful, the snow,' you say when you come in.

Hannah lifts her head to look at you, then looks down again at the tabletop.

'You could see it for yourself if you went outside.'

She shrugs. 'The snow isn't going anywhere.'

'Would you like some tea?'

By way of a response, she lifts the bottle to her mouth. She drinks slowly but greedily.

'Shall we play a game?'

There aren't any board games here, but you could come up with something: hangman or I spy. The kind of games you play with children to keep them quiet, to pass the time.

'Yes,' Hannah says, so loudly it makes you jump. 'Let's play a game. One where I ask the questions for a change.'

A normal conversation, a conversation between equals, rambles about, finding its own way. A therapeutic conversation is different. It has fixed boundaries you need to guard, to protect yourself and keep an eye on the bigger picture. It's common for the patient to rebel against these boundaries, offering resistance and demanding more, demanding access to your own life – the feeling they can do something for you too, or at least the suggestion of friendship. Normally, in the end, all the power stays in the hands of the therapist, because they can decide, if the worst comes to the worst, to stop the treatment, leaving the patient alone.

'How did your son die?' asks Hannah, still in that strange, harsh tone. 'Was he ill, did he have an accident? Did he disappear too? Did he commit suicide?'

You stare at your hands, not sure whether you can control your voice.

'Does it matter, to you? Is that important to you?'

'Yes.'

'You want to know how?'

'Maybe not how he died, but the fact he died. What happened to that boy, the boy in my class, it was so strange the way things went. People don't understand that, not if they've never experienced anything themselves, not something big.'

'Would it help you,' I ask, 'to imagine that boy was my son?'

She looks at you and you really think she's going to ask the question, you're almost hoping she will, but she doesn't say anything. Some silences can't be broken, some things can't be said aloud, even if they're so clearly present, so suffocating.

Later she apologises for her directness. 'But that's just the way I am.' She laughs a little, holding one hand in front of her mouth.

179

'At drama school they told us acting isn't therapy, but that's nonsense. Not because wallowing in emotions produces good theatre; it doesn't, they were right about that. But it can help cast out the demons and that was an experience I wanted my students, who never showed any emotions, to have.

'Sometimes I asked them what they were afraid of.

'I would ask the whole group and later I would ask them individually. Then they would start to laugh and say, "You don't think we'd tell you that?" They were always afraid of what would happen with the things they said and showed, scared that their openness would come back to them like a boomerang.

'Fear has an odour, true panic stinks. I smelled it on Kito. It must have been something in his sweat, a chemical adjustment. It's repellent, the smell of the underdog.

'Despite this, I arranged to meet with him more often, after the lesson had ended and the others had gone home. After that first time I'd offered to give him extra lessons, and he didn't dare refuse. He seemed happy with such a formal description of our meetings – he was one of those rare children who long for tasks and responsibilities. As long as he was in the classroom he was safe from his classmates.

'"Why do you make such an effort?" he asked me once. He was sitting on a table, his legs dangling, while I was packing up my things. His question sounded more reproachful than grateful.

'"You're worth making an effort for. Everyone is, when you come down to it."

'He stared at his shoes, which were leather and well-polished. "I meant the lessons, not what you do for me. You put such a lot of energy into them."

'I told him about my ideals, about the things drama can bring about. I said, "Sometimes pretending to be another person is the only way you can be yourself."

'"They laugh at you."

'I looked at the tabletop, and the messages carved into it with Stanley knives. Girls' names and phone numbers. *Call X for a blow job. Y woz here.*

'"I'm sure they laugh at all the teachers," I said calmly.

'"Not in the same way."

'He was looking me in the eye for the first time. His eyes were a very dark brown. I laughed uncomfortably. "What do they say?"

'He shifted about on the table. "You shouldn't trust Timothy."

'"I get along fine with Timothy."

'"He's playing with you."'

After a pause she went on: 'It's your body that decides whether or not to trust someone. Usually it happens in a split second, subconsciously. When Timothy was nearby your whole body would tense up. I saw it in the students but also, to my shame, in myself – the realization of what could happen. The threat lay in his expressionless gaze, the dangerously slippery surface of his emotions, the way his mood could suddenly turn, completely out of the blue.

'Sometimes, in passing, I felt his hand touch my bottom, always so fleetingly it was hard to make anything of it. I never protested, what could I have said without making bigger and more important than it was? It was better to pretend it was just an accidental collision between his body and mine, even though it repeated itself every lesson.

'Looking back it seems strange I didn't listen to Kito, or ask him what he meant. But I listened to him out of politeness and it was easy enough to put his words down to his own precarious situation. He was – how shall I put it – unformed. Maybe he'd had to hide for so long that he didn't know who he was anymore. There was nothing interesting or characteristic about him, he'd hidden all of that away. He didn't speak, he mumbled. He never looked you in the eye, which always made you feel he was holding something back. I tried to explain some things to him about acting, the basics. How you need to feel the meaning while you say the lines, what the difference is between acting and reciting, how the expression in your voice is always carried by your breath. He wanted to learn how to speak better, do presentations, and maybe that's why he kept sticking around.

'He told me, much later, that he spent every break in the toilets, writing notes to himself in his notebook, because there was no one to speak to. It's hard to imagine how completely kids that age are left at each other's mercy. Those are the things we forget when we look back on our own youth – the way a school is much like a totalitarian state. We say it's good for them, it builds character; we say they need to get used to it and then we turn away, stop listening to what they say. The thing you forget is how interminable a school day is,

182

and how there's nowhere to withdraw to apart from the toilets, where your predecessors have used pens and keys to leave their mark. I saw him sometimes, when I was early and he had a free period. He would be staring at the display cases with the trophies and medals that sporting heroes had won for the school long ago. He held his hands behind his back and peered at the labels. It was painfully obvious that these didn't really interest him, and he was just looking at them so he didn't have to turn around, or face the corridor. Not that this offered any real protection against the other students, who walked through the hallway in boisterous groups and nearly pushed him aside as they passed, clipping the back of his head or slapping him on the bum like they did with the girls. He never turned around and didn't react, he just looked at those trophies and the yellowing photos of the boys' teams. Each of those boys was his exact opposite: strong, athletic, self-assured.'

To save on firewood you sleep in the same room as Hannah, listening to the sound of her breathing at night. It doesn't sound like she's bothered by nightmares and thoughts; she usually sleeps well, her breathing even and her movements calm. Sleep opens up her face, making its lines look sculpted but fragile. Someone could put a pillow over her face. Then she'd resist, her limbs convulsing but ultimately powerless. It would be a relief not to have to look at her anymore, not to have to listen to what she tells you.

You dream of white dresses and one red one, the colour of rotting meat. You dream you're holding on to everything until you can't anymore, and then all

183

those things fall from your hands, melting and dripping through your fingers, and then you wake up.

Later you ask her, almost casually, 'You mentioned an incident.'

But she pretends not to hear or maybe she really hasn't heard, and you're afraid to repeat the question. 'You get fireflies here in summer,' she says. 'I don't know if you've seen them. When I'd just got here I couldn't get over how bright they were. Whole evenings I'd sit outside staring at those things glowing in the dark.

'At drama school they'd told me I needed to ground myself, and maybe that was all that was required. Now I was here, somewhere else, time would fold itself back and the world would restore itself. I remember so vividly how I hoped that would happen, and almost took it for granted. I kept imagining how I would be living here in a couple of years' time, completely self-sufficient. How I'd wander through the forest with a dog beside me, and ride a horse perhaps. In those dreams I never limped and of course I didn't know then what hard work it is to live like that, how hard it is when you haven't grown up with it. There are people who seem to have an in-built talent for these things; it's a knack or perhaps it's a question of confidence – I had neither, though. The only thing I could do was stare at those fireflies at night and maybe that was enough. Do you believe in reincarnation?'

'No.'

'It seems like it'd be a comforting thought. In your situation.'

You don't answer. There are so many nicer thoughts that are supposed to provide consolation, but that doesn't mean you can go ahead and believe in them, just because you want to. After Kito's announcement had appeared in the paper, strangers and acquaintances came to offer comfort. He wasn't dead, not really, but in heaven and safe and happy there. He wasn't dead but would come back to earth, may have been born again already. It was incredible to see how self-centred people were, how eager to use you to keep their own rose-tinted beliefs afloat.

'I believe in it,' Hannah says proudly. 'Maybe not after death, I don't know about that, nobody does after all, but I hope ...' She doesn't finish her sentence. 'But in life, yes; I believe you can become a completely different person. That you can decide to come into the world a second time, and it's your own choice, ultimately.'

You wonder if you were ever like that, the way she is now – so hopeful, so excruciatingly naïve.

Later that week friends of Hannah's drop by, Liam and Melanie and their daughter. When they were here in the summer, the little girl, a chubby toddler with blonde ringlets, had run around in circles like mad. She looked very cute then, with her plump little arms and a straw hat that kept falling off; now she's older and so pale it looks unhealthy. She kicks against the leg of the table and refuses to stop even after her parents warn her and scold her.

You bring coffee and the cake Hannah insisted you bake – 'Hospitality is the only rule here.' You make faces at the child, but she doesn't react, just stares at you with a serious expression. Liam and Melanie also seem more worn out than in the summer. They're thinking of going back. 'Not for long, just to get through the winter.'

They're talking about the situation in the rest of the country, the protests in the capital about rising energy prices, the poverty many Bulgarians live in. They're things you've heard about on the radio, but they have nothing to do with life here.

The girl coughs.

Hannah puts a bottle of *rakia* on the table and they start drinking. Liam talks about his plans to become rich by driving back and forth between Bulgaria and the West, making good money on things that are considered old rubbish over here. He has a second glass of *rakia* and then a third, even though earlier he said he was driving. The roads are icy now, the bends treacherous, and yet they stay until long after dark. Liam does most of the talking, while Melanie stares into space and smiles like it's hard work. When you get up to get another bottle, you can feel their eyes on your back. You're no longer this summer's volunteer, just passing through, but they're having trouble figuring out what you are instead, how they should relate to you. They ask you if you're thinking of buying a house too.

'No.'

The silence goes on a little too long. They're waiting for an explanation you don't give them, and the conversation doesn't really get going again after that.

After a while you get up and go to the door, putting your shoes on to go to the toilet. It's good to be alone and you stay outside for a long time, wrapping your arms around yourself against the cold. From the veranda you hear the others talking over each other, Liam's loud

186

voice and Melanie's shrill, cynical laugh. They fall silent when you come in and not long after Liam says they should be going. This is followed by the usual fussing around with scarves and winter coats, promises to drop by again soon and awkward hugs.

After the tail lights have disappeared, Hannah sinks back onto the sofa, her face suddenly empty and exhausted.

'They were worried about me.'

'Why?'

She sniffs. 'They think you have an unhealthy influence on me. They don't understand why you're still here, what you're doing here if you don't actually plan to stay here.'

'And what do you think?'

'I don't know what I'd do without you.'

Then she bursts out laughing. At first, you laugh along with her, but gradually her laughter becomes shriller and less controlled. You just stand there, holding a cup in your hand, while she doubles over, wiping the tears from her face.

The walls you whitewashed in the summer have already been covered again by a dark, greasy film of soot. You imagine, you don't even know why, that this is how things will always go: in the spring, Hannah will get up, you will whitewash the walls and then, in winter, they will once again become dirty and black.

When you're alone, you bite your nails to the quick.

What's the weight of something that's disappeared? How heavy can someone be when he's no longer there? You gave him what you could, what you had, but it

187

wasn't enough. You squeezed oranges for him every day, because it was good for him. One day, the core of one of the oranges was pitch-black, like a fire had raged within. You only noticed afterwards, though, when he was already holding the glass. Countless tiny, jet-black particles swirled around in the liquid, but he drank it down without looking. He always trusted you.

One morning you call Mark. Only when you're about to hang up does he answer. His voice sounds curt and businesslike, not the way you remembered it, not the way you'd hoped.

'Mark?'

For a moment, all you hear is his breathing, distorted, far away. You could have a conversation like this, without saying anything; maybe that's what you should do, renounce words and listen to the sounds of the body, breath and heartbeat.

'What are you doing there?' he asks. 'Why are you still there?'

His voice sounds hoarse, he's a little out of breath. You imagine he's just got off his bicycle, downed the contents of his water bottle in the kitchen and then picked up the phone.

'I'm worried,' he says. 'I didn't know whether to call the police, or what I should say if I did. I miss you.'

You're silent. You wonder if he cooks for himself, whether he lays the table.

'Can I reach you on this number?' he insists. 'Are you still there? When are you coming back?'

There's nothing to say and so you hang up, just like that, not giving him the chance to protest. Then you just stand there, listening to the monotonous sound of the phone telling you there's no one left. Still, this wasn't the actual separation but, at most, the confirmation of something that had already happened, or that's what you tell yourself as you walk back to the house.

'With him, Kito I mean,' Hannah says, 'it was like approaching a shy animal, a bird or a mouse or some other tiny, nervous creature. I could get nearer, but only if I did it so slowly and so carefully it seemed like I wasn't moving towards him at all. Once you start doing that, it becomes a kind of art in itself, a pastime, even if the animal in question doesn't really interest you that much.

'At the start of each lesson I had the students do an exercise to loosen them up, and one time I picked the exaggeration circle. It's a simple idea: one person walks around the classroom in circles and the rest watches. That's scary enough at that age, but then it gets worse. Someone starts walking behind you and exaggerating your movements, just a little to start with. You're not allowed to look behind you, not even when the class starts laughing. Then someone else starts walking behind that person, exaggerating a little more and so on, until you have the whole group following you. That's when you're allowed to step out of the line and look at what has become a caricature of yourself, a brazen amplification of everything your mother used to warn you about. Maybe you walk around with your back slightly bent or your head sticking out in front or you have a dopey grin on your face. All those things, all your habits, are mercilessly put on display.

189

'I'd done the exercise before during my placements, but always with groups of adults, people who were doing my course for pleasure. Each time, it was only when we'd started – too late – that I noticed how radically different this kind of exercise worked in a group of secondary-school students. They were ruthless in the way they copied each other's defects, and mine too, and I could only look on as Timothy exaggerated my limp and made fun of me. He dragged his left leg along the floor, his entire body skewed by the deformity he simulated, with a semi-imploring look on his twisted face. The terrifying thing was that I recognized myself in him, he was acting out all the things I didn't want to be – not just the disability but everything associated with it, the way people either turn away or look at you for too long, their self-conscious effort to act normal. He had enough control over his face, usually so impassive, to truly turn into a version of me. Just once, he looked in my direction and held my gaze. It was no coincidence, he knew what he was doing and was enjoying it. But I couldn't stop the exercise now; his victory would be obvious. I just stood there while the kids nudged each other and started laughing louder and louder. They looked at me, all of them, and all I wanted was to walk out of the classroom and never come back. But I knew they'd stare at my leg and that was the only thing that kept me standing there. That's the moment I decided things needed to change.'

She said, 'There's one thing you always need to remember: the fact that they listen to you and do what

190

you say is just an agreement. And that agreement can be broken at any time, stealthily or with brute violence.

'Not every student is capable of it; many of them won't want to. But nearly every class has one kid whose status depends on their disdain for the rules, which they have to demonstrate again and again to retain their air of invulnerability, and the glamour that comes with it. Maybe those kids know it too, that at this point they have not yet failed, something that often happens soon after they leave school. Maybe they know that these years are their years, and of course they're often desperate and powerless at home.

'That makes them terrifying at school. Sometimes, if you don't get in their way too much, it's possible to get through the school year in one piece, and even come to something you could call an understanding with them. When you know you're the weakest you avoid that confrontation, you put up with it. You put up with it so long because you hope to keep your dignity intact, more or less. You adapt. The threat never really disappears, but you can live with it, if you don't make them look ridiculous and don't ask them for their input too often.

'Until they feel the need for a new demonstration. At that moment, the conflict that was always there suddenly comes out into the open for everyone to see, and you will have to act and show them who's strongest. I saw Timothy's father once, a man in combat boots and a bomber jacket, his hair gelled back straight over his skull. The Rottweiler he had with him followed his commands very obediently and whenever I saw Timothy after that I always thought of that dog and the submissive look in its eyes.

'I'd put up and shut up the whole term, and I'd been prepared to carry on like that till the last lesson. Now, on the spot, I decided to challenge them. "Imagine," I said, "portraying the opposite of the way you normally are. We have Richard's words, we have Shakespeare's text. When you learn those by heart" – a collective groan – "when you learn them by heart and you say them, then that's all we have: the way you are all the time, with the emotions everyone knows and using them to act out an old, dead text. But I want you to expand your repertoire. I want you to say those lines like you're someone else, or rather a different version of yourself. One you don't know yet. So, for example, for Timothy to say those lines in a very loving way. What would that take? Are you familiar with that emotion, Timothy? Love?"

'Laughter. Timothy looked around, his face pale with anger, his mouth a narrow line. We waited, the students and me too, but he didn't say anything and after a while things went quiet. Now there was nobody who dared laugh openly, but every now and then somebody would start giggling and then stop quickly.

'"Love, Timothy. I think that would be a really good assignment for you, to do this monologue and take love as your starting point. And the same goes for all of you: choose an emotion you don't use very often. You'll prepare it at home and present it in the last lesson."

'They picked up their bags and left the classroom accompanied by the customary noise, Kito being the only one to stay behind as usual. I put the tables back and wiped the board. It was only after they'd gone that I realized what I'd done, and the thought scared me.

'"Hey," I said to Kito. "Hey, what about a bit of singing?"

'He stared at me.

'I connected my iPod to the speakers and scrolled through the list looking for a suitable song, one of those tear-jerkers everyone likes to listen to now and then although they'd never admit to it. "The point is," I said, "that you have to really believe in it. So when I sing 'I love you', you should be able to hear it's true. Even if it isn't. Or is, but in a different way, at another level."

'No reaction.

'I put the music on and walked to the middle of the classroom. I made a fist, holding it under my mouth like a microphone, and sang, "You belong to me, you make me happy. You be-lo-hoong to me, you make my life complete."

'The trick is to get over your embarrassment and put some actual feeling into the tacky and sentimental lyrics, making them real in the process. It can take a while before you manage it. The comic aspect of a performance like that is clear from the start though, and even Kito was starting to smile a little. Encouraged, I aimed my words directly at him, walking over to him and looking into his eyes, loudly drawing out the notes: "You be-lo-hoong to meee."

'He giggled.

'He looked away, then back. His giggling got louder while I kept a straight face, making him laugh even louder. It was the kind of game you could have played with a much younger child and we carried on like that for a while, but then I hit a deeper layer. My voice shifted, becoming lower and more grounded.

Kito felt the change as well. I was still aiming the lyrics at him and he was listening, serious now, with a hint of compassion in his large brown eyes. When the music stopped I was still standing there. I made an awkward bow. He didn't clap but stood up and solemnly shook my hand, a strange gesture for someone his age.

'That afternoon I didn't go straight home but cycled into town to buy something, some item that would make me feel like I was someone else, the kind of woman that makes people turn their heads in the street, and not because of her limp. I wandered past the windows and finally went into a shoe shop. I usually wore sensible, flat shoes which didn't tax my leg too much. That afternoon I saw a pair of colourful boots with high heels. Happiness was a choice too, I thought, admiring myself in the shop's mirrors. You had to feel you deserved it, fake it if you had to.'

'There are guidelines of course,' Hannah went on, 'rules saying what you are and aren't supposed to do as a teacher. Male teachers these days make sure they're never alone in a classroom with a girl; everyone's heard the stories. But I always thought the boundaries would be clear-cut, defined.'

She must have seen the expression on your face, because she carries on before you can say anything. 'It wasn't anything like that, don't get me wrong. Even now, as I'm telling you, I still don't know what someone else would call it. But at the time I wasn't thinking about that, I was just doing what seemed right.'

'The new boots forced my left leg in an uncomfortable position, and by the end of the next lesson my feet were so sore that I had to kick them off, even though Kito was still in the classroom, lingering as usual. He'd already spent more than five minutes packing his school bag, which I thought was quite an achievement.

'I was leaning forward on my chair, massaging my feet, and from the corner of my eye I could see him staring at the boots, which were bright red and almost slutty. There was something obscene about the way they lay there, the zips undone and the lining visible. Looking back, I'm amazed I asked him that question, but sometimes all it takes for someone to become a clown is to put on the nose or the suit. "Would you like to try them on? I think they might fit you."

'He was silent.

'But he kept looking at the boots.

'"Just try them," I repeated.

'He still didn't move.

'It would be a role for him to try out, a disguise. It was no more than that, a game – something to seduce him into acting, if he ever had it in him at all. "I bought them to look taller, but one must suffer to be beautiful."

'There was no reaction.

'"What's your size anyway?"

'He walked up to the boots to check the size, but not before he'd made sure no one was outside, and no classmates hanging around. He passed the shoes from one hand to the other, running his fingers along the bright-red leather.

195

'He sat there like that for a long time. A few times I thought he was about to lay the boots aside. A sudden, abrupt movement, like he wanted to force himself to get up and break the spell. But the shame he felt wasn't strong enough.

'From where I was sitting, a few metres away, I watched the conflict playing out on his face. It was a struggle I didn't understand, although I thought I did then. I was happy when he finally seemed to make a decision, picking up one of the boots to put it on.

'The boots looked ridiculous on him. It was like that game where everyone draws a different section of a person without knowing what the others have done. Someone had given him bright-red women's boots, while another person had drawn the stuffy, straight-legged trousers and the overly serious expression. He was made up of disparate parts but he wasn't aware of it.

When he'd put on both boots he straightened his back and stood there. He wobbled a little, then regained his balance.

'He didn't look at me and I didn't try to meet his eye either. I didn't say anything, just watched and waited.

'He took a few tentative steps, like a foal trying out its long legs for the first time. Looking back it's difficult to describe what happened, how he changed while walking through the classroom like that. Stumbling about at first, his awkwardness was endearing, and he kept looking up at me. But then he seemed to retreat to a place deep inside himself, the expression on his face withdrawn but calm, serene. Suddenly the boots didn't look quite so ridiculous.

'I looked at him in surprise, thinking of the boy I'd seen in my lessons. The effort he made to speak clearly, and the pitiful mumbling this produced. How he was constantly censuring himself, even before he said a word, his posture weighed down by a sadness that had already crystallized.

'When does someone turn into the one who is always picked on?

'I asked a few colleagues if they knew anything about his parents, his home situation. All I knew was that he lived in one of those expensive houses near the dunes. Unlike Timothy, Kito was hardly ever the subject of conversations in the staffroom, although some teachers knew his father, who did something important to do with development aid and had given a presentation on the topic for the older classes. Every time I looked at him I wondered how a child could have got so very lost. But perhaps this was what his parents wanted, what they saw as a proper upbringing: this kind of affected, stifling politeness.'

The whole time she is talking you imagine a sound in the background, a high-pitched tone accompanying her words, making them bearable. There are therapies based on this principle. The traumatized patient relives their memory but stays connected to the present through sounds. You never really believed in it, not in the revolution it was claimed to represent – probably what helped the patients was telling their story in a safe environment. But still it's tempting to surrender to that sound, to let it swallow up her voice, her questions and her comments.

It's customary for the mother to get the blame, you've heard it often enough from your patients. Mothers set the boundaries, marking out the space in which you become a person. Resistance is possible, much later, but only of a marginal kind. You yourself never became the doctor your mother hoped you would. As a teenager you'd already changed in a way that she, despite all her efforts, may have always known she couldn't prevent. There were boys, she was sure, and you were rotten on the inside, already dirty, a slut. You learnt to act like you couldn't hear her, but you couldn't keep her words from finding their way in and nestling deep inside your body. You'd never been touched by anyone.

'I don't have any children, of course,' Hannah says. 'So maybe it's easier for you to understand – what happens when they grow up, how they distance themselves. Maybe you can tell me about that some time.'

There was that one time at the pool when he wanted to show you how well he could swim on his back. It surprised you because the swimming lessons were a disaster, which he endured bravely but with no enthusiasm whatsoever. But then he asked you to come and you did. He called 'Look, Mama, look,' and you watched him turn on his back and swim towards the deep end. Before he got there, he started to disappear underwater. Despite this, he kept going, making the same movements, only with his head, his mouth and nose under water. You wanted to help him, reach out and support his back, but you didn't; he needed to learn to do it by himself, become more independent. So you kept watching as the water covered his serious face and his closed eyes. You were already reaching out when

198

he suddenly turned over and, gasping, came up to the surface. When he'd recovered enough to talk, he said, 'I was gone, wasn't I, Mama?' He sounded frightened and it was only then you remembered your own lessons when you were a girl, the endless depths of the water below you, and how terrifying it was.

So you lifted him out of the water and dried him in your large towel, his smooth skin under your hands, hugging him until he protested he wasn't a baby anymore, and then you bought him an ice cream, whichever one he wanted, but it wasn't enough. You should have supported him, but instead you just stood there waiting, watching while he almost drowned.

You don't say any of this, it's not your story that's the issue here. And after you let the silence go on long enough she starts up again, as you knew she would.

'He was wearing those boots, he was someone completely different. I have no idea how long he stood there. The feeling of concentration was so intense I could hear every detail: the cars outside, a telephone that kept ringing in the staffroom. At one point it looked like he was going to cry, and I stood up to walk over to him. This made him aware of my presence again and, moving too suddenly, he lost his balance.

'This broke the spell.

'He bent over to unzip the boots, kicking them off like they'd burnt him. Without looking at me again, he put his own brown lace-ups back on, got his bag and jacket and stumbled out of the classroom and into the corridor. I wanted to go after him, to ask him what had happened, which I didn't understand myself. Looking back, that's what I should have done, or at least tried, even if I could never have caught up with him with my leg. But I was too scared someone might see me, limping along in my stockinged feet.

'At that moment, everything could still have turned out differently. It could have remained a one-off experiment, a joke – although we both knew it wasn't. We could have chosen not to mention it again and then it would have faded, it wouldn't have acquired any significance.

'But the next lesson I took him aside and said, "The only thing that matters is that you can be yourself here. That may not be possible or allowed anywhere else, but it is here. In this classroom it's safe, you can be who you really are."

'I don't even know if I was talking to him or mainly to myself, and I couldn't tell whether my words were making any kind of impression. He said nothing, just tried, as always, to escape from the intimacy as quickly as he could. But later he said those same words I'd heard him say a hundred times – "Is there a murderer here? No. Yes, I am." – and for the first time I heard something different there, a deeper layer he hadn't shown before during the lessons. Or maybe I was able to see him differently now.

'The way I'm telling it makes it sound like cross-dressing maybe, but I don't think that's what it was. He was trying out versions of himself. He was looking for a form that hadn't been appropriated by others. That serious boy with the brown shoes and corduroy trousers was someone else's ideal, maybe he never really existed. He tried so hard though.

200

'There were things he and I didn't talk about, subjects that remained off limits, like his family. He did mention there was no one waiting for him in the afternoons, that his parents didn't come home until around dinnertime.

'"So what do you do when you're home alone?"

'He shrugged.

'"Just watch TV. Do some drawing."

'"Drawing?"

'He gave me a quick, sideways glance.

'"What do you draw?"

'"I don't know. Just things."

'"Would you show me one of your drawings?"

'"Why?"

'"Because I'm curious to see what you draw."

'"Why?"

'Talking to him was a bit like playing chess: making moves, coming up with manoeuvres to draw him out. "Is it so strange someone might be interested in what you come up with?"

'"Not here," he said, and I nearly laughed, just stopping myself in time when I saw how offended he looked. "You can see them, but not at school."

'"Where then?"

He thought for a moment. "In the dunes."

'"Kito, I can't just – you understand that, right?"

'"OK, suit yourself," he said.

'At that moment I could have followed the rules, I could have told him that something like that was out of the question. That would have been the sensible thing. But the newspaper cuttings in my room showed me every day the damage that is done by people who follow the rules and stay within the system. Should I have left him hanging just when he was showing me a tentative glimpse of what was hidden so deep inside him?

'"OK, the dunes it is. When?"

'"Tomorrow."

'And so the day after I found myself walking behind him along a narrow path through the dunes, like we were conspirators. Every now and then he would stop to point out the sound of a blue tit, a chaffinch or a thrush. He seemed to know the names of all the birds and exactly where he was going. I wondered how much time he'd spent there in the dunes, how many of those lone afternoons.

'As if he could hear my thoughts, he turned around and said, "I slept out here once, alone, in a sleeping bag, and when I woke up they were all sitting around me, all the little birds you get here. Because I was lying there without moving they hadn't noticed I was a human being and they came really close, but of course when I moved they were startled and flew off right away. It still surprised me though, because it felt like they'd chosen me, the way it happens in fairy tales."

'I was about to reply when he put a finger to his lips, pointing at a deer not far ahead; it looked straight at us for a second, before leaping into the bushes and disappearing.

'I couldn't quite shake off a sense of enchantment, an irrational idea that animals weren't as scared of him – but maybe it was just because he'd learnt to make himself invisible at school.

'Finally, he left the path, leading me along a new, meandering route under the trees, courteously holding branches aside.

'"We're not far from the beach," he said. "If you listen carefully you can hear the sea."

'We stood there for a moment and then he turned towards me.

'"If I ever die this is where I want to be buried. Not under a stone, and I don't want to be cremated either. I'd rather disappear into nothing very slowly and finally turn into a tree a bird can sit on, or this grass here, waving at the sea."

'I turned my head to look at him. The sun shone on his cheeks and his eyes were closed. I didn't know if it was normal for him to be able to talk about death like it was a long-lost friend. I didn't know if that was normal for teenagers – I thought of the way I used to fantasize about my own funeral. Maybe I should have told someone, but I didn't know who to tell, or if it would be a betrayal. I didn't know how seriously I should take him. What do you know about death at that age, how real and irreversible it is?

'"Are you coming for a swim?" he asked, standing up and beating the sand off his legs.

'"I'm not that keen on swimming."

'But he didn't hear me and started running. I stood there for a moment, watching his figure grow smaller.

'"Are you coming or what?" he called from the top of the dune, cupping his hands round his mouth.

'Climbing up the dune, my feet made hollows in the shifting sand that immediately filled up again. I had

203

none of his lightness and speed. He waited for me a moment longer, then hurtled down the slope, his arms milling about as he ran across the beach, right up to the sea. I also waved my arms about and shouted like he did, but it wasn't real and I stopped before I even got to the beach. I couldn't keep up with him anyway.

'He wasn't looking back anymore.

'He was splashing through the surf and then let himself fall forward onto the water. I watched him. He'd told me about his fears, how scared he was that all the things he did or thought would have serious consequences. He'd already caused one person's death, he said – his real mother had died when he was born.'

You interrupt her. 'I can't believe you went to the dunes with one of your students, alone.'

Normally in a therapeutic situation it's not about what really happened. The only thing that matters is how the patient experienced the past, or rather, how they experience it now, at this point in their lives. It's not important whether that experience, the story of their life, is correct, because who's in a position to say? The only thing that matters is whether the patient can make peace with that history, no longer seeing it as a disruptive force, and experience themselves as whole.

Other rules are at work here; getting to the truth is a matter of life and death. You're not interrupting her because you don't believe her, though. On the contrary, you're afraid it's true. He showed her a place you never saw and that's why you're protesting, even though you can hear how weak it sounds.

'I think it's irresponsible, as a teacher.'

It's the first time you've put aside the role of therapist, but she doesn't seem to notice. Maybe she doesn't need you as an audience anymore, maybe she doesn't look up to you anymore. Very soon now you will have to make a decision, carry out the deed.

Finish it.

Hannah said: 'Later that afternoon he led me to a spot you couldn't see from the path. Suddenly I asked myself what I was doing there with him in the middle of the dunes. I hadn't told a soul where I was. I remembered my conversation with Astrid in the bike shed, and how he'd been listening.

'"I should be getting home."

'But he'd already taken a sketchpad out of his bag and handed it to me rather solemnly, before fishing out a bottle of squash. It really was squash, not one of those brightly coloured energy drinks his classmates preferred, and that made me laugh.

'"Private joke," I said, when he looked at me suspiciously.

'It's surprising how childish drawings by boys that age can be, how awkward. Almost endearing, like their handwriting. Kito had passed that stage and had gone further than many of his classmates ever would, but he hadn't found his style yet. His drawings were hesitant and sometimes clumsy, but they contained the promise of the artist he could become.

'All his sketches depicted women. Women with dresses that merged into two wings on their backs, or with a train that curved upwards, turning into a flock of colourful birds. Women with complicated hairdos

205

constructed from shiny feathers. They had heavy eyebrows and full lips, and eyes that seemed to long for some place out of their reach.

'Kito took a cheap cake from his bag, and used a knife to cut it into slices. He looked at me expectantly, hopefully.

'"They're beautiful pictures, Kito, really beautiful."

'He looked past me, waiting.

'"Is there a special meaning to your drawings, Kito? Is there something you're trying to say?"

'"What do you think?" he asked nervously. "Don't you like them?"

He'd picked a stalk of grass and as we talked he was tying it into knots, one after the other.

'"Yes, I do, I said so, didn't I? They're very beautiful."

'He clenched his fists and then stretched his fingers out again. He was sitting so close to me I could hear his breathing.

'"You're an artist, a real artist."

He frowned.

'"Don't you recognize anything?"

'I looked at the drawings again, for longer this time. His lines weren't perfect, lacked the precision that comes with years of practice, and it was the way he was staring at me more than the drawings themselves that suddenly made me realize that it was me he'd been drawing, that all those women were representations of me.

'"Have you ever shown these to anyone else?"

'He didn't answer, but took the sketchpad and snapped it shut, carefully wrapping it in plastic before putting it back in his bag. I thought it was over, the moment had passed – and I had failed. But he didn't get up, offering me another piece of cake instead, which I accepted and put in my mouth, even though I'd had enough. It's funny how you remember odd details; how the cake was marbled with a swirl of something passing for chocolate, its spongy taste. I could hear myself chewing and was ashamed of the sounds, all the more so because he'd stopped eating and was just staring at me admiringly.

'It dawned on me again how ridiculous the situation was, with us sitting there like two little children. I wanted to get up and leave, but just at that moment he stretched out his hand. I thought maybe there was a wasp or some other insect he wanted to bat away. But instead he put his hand on the side of my head, took a strand of my hair and, almost reverentially, tucked it back behind my ear. He didn't look me in the eye.

'He was too old to be doing this, or maybe too young. He no longer had the privileges of a child that doesn't know any better, but neither did he have an adult's right to determine their own life. He was still so serious he was starting to scare me, and this seriousness made it impossible to ignore him, or to dismiss the gesture with a joke. Instead, I shook him off roughly and limped away through the buckthorn bushes, as fast as I could, past rows of trees, looking like the bars of a cage in the evening mist that had appeared too quickly. I was waiting for him to follow me or call out to me, and I was relieved to see the first houses and the lights burning inside. I stayed there for a long time under the plane trees, staring at the people moving about in the villas. But no matter how long I stood there watching, imagining their lives, they remained shadowy figures. They never became real.

'I waited for him for a while longer. I thought he'd be coming any minute now and it felt different here, with houses around and lights nearby. I wanted to say I was sorry for the way I reacted, and how happy I was to see the things he showed me and that I felt honoured. But he didn't come and eventually I got cold and went home, telling myself he must have taken a different route home, getting back long before I did.

'We were nearing the end of the term and the school had said nothing about extending my contract. With the summer holidays round the corner, the students were even more difficult to control and no one was really in the mood for the performance I'd promised them at the start of our lessons. In the end, the school wasn't prepared to help either, not even by making the auditorium available.

'"Take them to the beach," Van Eeteren suggested. "An outing, it'll do you all good. You can do something there, just for the group. Have a barbecue as well, see it as a team-building thing."

'I protested, but it was no use, and in the end it didn't seem such a bad idea to me. By now I realized at least half of the parents wouldn't bother to turn up to a performance, while the students would only attend if they got marks for it, and would behave accordingly. When I suggested the idea in class a loud cheer went up; no one even mentioned the performance or seemed to remember it had ever been on the cards.

'Kito was the only one who remained silent, but there was nothing unusual about that. I had wanted to take him aside before the lesson to apologize and explain to him why I'd run away, that I never should have gone with him. But, contrary to his habit, he came in last, so I had no choice but to start the lesson.

'I asked the students to run around as fast as they could, in no fixed pattern. It's an exercise that trains alertness, the kind of concentration dancers or actors need to carry out coordinated movements without being able to see each other. They ran around like mad people, bumping into each other accidentally on purpose. In the process, Kito fell to the floor several times after someone had given him a shove. Then he would get up and start running again, staring vacantly. Once I thought I saw he had his eyes closed.

'Eventually I asked them to stop and after repeating myself four or five times they listened, gathering on one side of the classroom, laughing. "Today I want to do a very special exercise with you. Today I want you to lift up one of your classmates while you say your lines."

'There was a collective groan.

'"Just try it," I said, sounding more upbeat than I felt. "You'll find it helps you feel the words in your body. Timothy, maybe you can go first and show the class. Kito can be your partner."

'"Do I have to?" Timothy asked. "I'd rather lift Samantha."

'It was rather forced, of course, and irresponsible too. But time was running out. I wouldn't be at that school for much longer and I was still looking for a way in, something that would force Kito to make contact with someone else.

'"It's very important that you let Timothy carry all your weight," I said to Kito, who came forward with

209

visible reluctance. "Let him do the work. And Timothy, remember to lift from your knees."

'The boys stood next to each other awkwardly, keeping a careful distance while the class waited. "Come on then," I said, finally.

'Kito took one careful step in Timothy's direction. Timothy was staring at him with a disgusted look on his face.

'"Hurry up," I said.

'After what seemed an eternity, Kito was finally standing in front of Timothy, who held out his arms stiffly.

'"Kiss! Kiss!" the class shouted.

'It clearly cost Timothy a great deal of effort to lift Kito up; it must have been a matter of prestige. He managed to stand up straight with Kito in his arms, but when he started to speak it was through clenched teeth: "Is there a murderer here? No. Yes, I am: then fly. What, from myself?"

'The struggle added a greater charge and weight to every word.

'After a while his arms started trembling, but he kept on speaking with Kito hanging there in front of his chest, avoiding everyone's eyes. Immediately after he'd spoken the last sentence, Timothy let go of Kito, who fell to the floor and got up directly to hide away somewhere near the edge of the room.

'"You've seen how it works," I said to the class, but they were all looking at Timothy, who was holding his hands in the air triumphantly, like a boxer.

'At the end of the lesson Kito was the first to leave the classroom. There were things I'd wanted to say to him, about the exercise and how there'd been some kind of

210

contact at least. I'd wanted to give him hope that things would get better.

'I'd invited all the teachers to our presentations at the beach, but only Astrid had turned up. She stayed and watched for a while. She wore orthopaedic sandals that showed her knobbly feet.

'"By now you all know Richard's monologue off by heart," I said. "And I asked you to consider this presentation as an invitation to explore a completely different side of yourself. We are now going to see what you discovered."

'Astrid and I were the only ones clapping loudly after each monologue.

'"The last one I'd like to invite over here is Timothy."

'Whistling from the crowd.

'Timothy stepped forward, turned to face the group and took a mocking bow.

'He cleared his throat loudly.

'Instantly there was silence.

'"Timothy," I said, "will present the monologue from a specific emotion, won't you, Timothy? We're interested to see the love you're going to show us."

'There was jeering, and he turned and grinned at his hecklers, ignoring me.

'Everyone knows the moment when an actor turns within, that brief, silent pause that marks the transition between real life and acting. In Timothy, the transition was seamless: one second he was himself, the next Richard III. He gave a convincing performance of a cunning, criminal king and that was an achievement in itself; he hadn't carried out the assignment though.

'Despite this, predictably, the class rewarded him with enthusiastic applause. Grinning, he bowed several times.

'"That was very good," I said, "but was it love? Is this the best you can do when it comes to love? Do you think anybody would believe you, is this coming from the bottom of your heart? Could you do better, do you have more to give?"

'The gob of spit hit me before I even saw it.

'"Bitch," he said, and then he spat again, right next to my feet this time, before walking away. I wiped the saliva from my face and tried to smile. Shortly after, Astrid said she had to go, walking off with large strides.

'Of course he came back.

'He came back and rejoined the group and we all pretended nothing had happened. His friends patted him on the back, that was all.

'Everyone had had their turn and the students seemed relieved to leave Richard behind them, along with all the complicated feelings he represented. The girls stretched out on bath towels, pushing aside the straps of their bikini tops to get an even tan. Someone had brought a ball; a game of football started up. I stood on the side watching for a while, before stepping forward to join in. They cheered ecstatically when I scored a goal, even though it was an accident, resulting from a mistake by the goalie.

'Around dusk, the first of the students started leaving. They checked their phones and said they had other, more urgent dates to keep: their parents, sports team or other friends who wanted to see them.

'But there was a small group that stayed. Someone gathered dry pieces of wood and a fire was lit by boys who wanted to show off their skills. The papers I'd handed out during the lessons also served as kindling, but they gave me a sidelong glance before setting them alight. I reassured them. "What I wanted to teach you should now be in your heads, not on those pieces of paper."

'The evening was too lovely to make a problem out of anything. It was exceptionally warm and even my impending unemployment didn't seem so problematic, or at least seemed far off. A couple of the girls were roasting marshmallows and handing them to their friends; someone was playing a bongo he'd brought from home – all of it harmless, old-fashioned fun. Maybe it was this place, the lack of walls around us, or just their expectations, with the summer holiday just around the corner. Someone had brought sausages, which they roasted over the fire, the grease dripping from the cheap meat sizzling in the flames.

'Maybe if I'd been closer or if I'd noticed earlier. If I'd understood what was happening at that moment, if I'd been on time to shout out – but why would they have listened to me at that point? Still, those are the questions you ask yourself, once it's happened and it's too late. When all you can do is stare at the wreckage, but you keep thinking how things could have gone, all the thousands of ways in which the bad thing could have been avoided. What's hardest to understand is how suddenly a beautiful night can turn into something you only see in films.

'I don't know who suggested it in the end. Timothy would seem the obvious person, and I can almost hear him say it now, but maybe it was someone else, maybe it wasn't even one of the boys. Whoever it was, they didn't put it as a question and the group didn't seem surprised either. They all seemed to have been waiting for this moment.

'I hadn't caught what was said at first but then Samantha repeated it: "Skinny dipping!"

'"OK, maybe we should skip that idea, guys?" I said.

'"You a bit of a prude, Hannah?"

'Laughter.

'"I just don't think it's such a good idea."

'"Or can't you swim, with that leg of yours?"

'They'd already started to take their clothes off.

'Of course I should have stopped them, but what's the worst that could happen, why spoil the evening by clinging to my role of teacher? I couldn't stop them anyway. If they didn't go swimming here and now they'd do it later, or a little further along, and here at least I could keep an eye on things. And there really wasn't that much difference between the girls' skimpy bikini's and not wearing anything at all. But these were all thoughts I came up with afterwards.

'"Not too far out," I said weakly, when they were already running towards the sea, "we won't go too far."

'But nobody was listening and they soon disappeared into the water with a lot of splashing about, their pale skin contrasting with the sky.

'The whole evening, Kito had been sitting to one side, his arms hugging his drawn-up knees.

'He hadn't said anything and no one had spoken to him, but nobody had picked on him or called him names either, not as far as I'd noticed anyway. It was pretty remarkable he'd stayed on in the first place, now that the official part was over. I tried to make contact, but he pretended not to see me and I gave up after a while.

'Now he was the only one sitting there by the fire with me, fiddling about with one of his toenails.

'"You could join them," I said. "You could go in the water too."

'We stared at the others, their heads the only things visible above water.

'"It's all gone really well, hasn't it?" I said. "You can be proud of what you've achieved in these lessons. Hasn't it turned out better than you expected, looking back?"

'He shrugged. He looked so lost. Suddenly the voices of the others sounded distorted and far away.

'"You have to keep going, Kito," I told him. "You mustn't hide yourself away."

'"What'll you do after the holidays?"

'"I don't know myself yet." I tried to laugh, but he didn't join in, just stared at me until I lowered my gaze.

'"You make people uncomfortable when you look at them like that – do you know that?"

'This was the last evening and I had no way of getting through to him, he was just as closed off as he had been during those first lessons. We'd spent so much extra time together, I'd done my best for him and now it seemed like all of that had gone to waste or wasn't important anymore. It was like I was a stranger to him. He let the sand trickle through his fingers, indifferent, no longer listening to what I was saying.

'When I looked up again, the sea had changed.

'In the spot where the kids were swimming the seawater was glowing with a fluorescent light. The colour was so bright it startled me. For a moment I thought of something chemical, a strange kind of pollution. I wanted to call out to them to get out, and then I thought maybe they'd emptied something into the water themselves, something they'd brought from home, a joke of some sort. Then I looked again and saw they were as surprised as I was, calling out to each other, waving their limbs about to see the effect. That's when I understood it had to be something in the sea itself, a type of seaweed maybe, or algae. I nudged Kito and he looked up too. I heard his sharp intake of breath.

'"Go in," I said. "Go on, it's too beautiful not to."

'He looked at me questioningly and so I said it again, more forcefully this time.

'"Get over there, enjoy yourself for a change. This is the best time of your life, it passes by so quickly."

'Very slowly, he took off his long trousers, revealing the swimming trunks he had on underneath. "Join in with them," I said. "It's really not that hard."

'I wanted to give him this, and maybe I wanted to give it to myself too, the memory of this night. One where he wasn't on the outside but one of the group, and for once he could act the way he was supposed to at his age. He threw his clothes on the ground and looked back at me one more time.

'"Go on," I said. "They won't bite. It's up to you."

'Then he started running, more gracefully than I'd expected, and I thought of the day he'd run to the sea swinging his arms around. I half expected him to shout ecstatically the way he did then.

'But all I heard was the sound of his footsteps disappearing and the shrieks of the others in the distance. I stayed there, sitting beside the dying embers and feeling old, like someone who belonged to a different world than theirs. Kito's arrival was greeted with shouts. At first he remained standing there at a short distance, but soon he was surrounded by the group. Ultimately these things depend on context and, of course, time; in a few more years the kids would settle down and there would be a lot less bullying.

'"He's wearing trunks," someone shouted. "That perv's wearing swimming trunks."

'There was laughter. I listened to their cheerful shrieks and watched them horse around while that strange light kept lapping around them.'

Hannah stops.

She can't stop now – you look at her, wanting to drag the words from her throat.

'And then?' you ask. 'What happened next?'

Your voice is shrill, and you're no longer the psychiatrist you've been playing, nor the bosom friend or the surrogate mother. You are no longer any of those things or maybe you never were.

'What happened then?' you ask again, and all you are is someone who's falling apart and she stares at you, surprised but not shocked. 'What happened to him then, how did it happen?', and it isn't a question and yet it is, it's the first and only question. 'What happened to him then, how did he disappear?'

Right now you're capable of attacking her, of tearing open her throat with your bare hands.

'That night,' she says, 'when I got back home, I stood in front of the mirror for a long time and slapped my bare belly, breasts and legs until they turned red. Then I covered myself up again quickly, ashamed. I held the kitchen scissors up to my braid and it was like I could feel the metal yearning to cut my hair. I felt a physical desire to punish myself, to leave a mark that would show what I had done, or had failed to do, but I didn't have the nerve. When I was little, my mother would brush my hair, slowly and carefully so as not to hurt me. Now that braid seemed like the only thing tethering me to the ground, as if its weight, accumulated over the years, was the only thing keeping me from just drifting off.

'At some point, I don't know how much time had passed, the noises changed. The voices sounded shriller and more fanatical. When I looked up I saw them pushing Kito underwater. It wasn't a game, it was too systematic.

'"Hey!" I called out, running over to the water. "Hey, stop that." They didn't hear me and I shouted louder. "Stop that I said!"

'My voice caught and I still wasn't sure they'd heard me over the sound of the waves. I screamed again, until I saw Timothy look up. He was staring at me, I don't know for how long, staring at me while he pushed Kito's head underwater and held it there.

'There was nothing I could do, I just stood there watching, but I couldn't move, scared to go into the water. Kito's head came up and was pushed under again and the rest did nothing either – the other kids seemed to have moved away, grouping together, unsure of themselves, leaving Timothy on his own. After what seemed to be an eternity he pulled Kito back up. They came out of the water, making a lot of noise now, as if a spell had been lifted, and Timothy had his arm around Kito's shoulders.

'Brushing past me, he stopped a moment, and I took an involuntary step backwards.

'"It was just a joke, *Hannah*."

'Kito bent over, retching, and Timothy, who was still holding on to him, gave him a hard slap on the back. "Just a little joke."

'Not long after the kids gathered up their things and trudged over to the entrance to the beach where they'd parked their bikes. Kito and I stayed behind next to the fire, which was slowly dying.

'I was scared to look him in the eye.

'He'd put a towel around his shoulders, but he hadn't dried himself off; he just sat there, huddled and shaking. "Are you all right, Kito?" I asked. "Are you OK?"

'He gave no sign of having heard me. "Is there anything I can do for you?"

'I sat there beside him for a while, but he didn't say a word all that time and I was afraid he didn't want me there – that he'd rather be alone. So in the end I left. I wished him good luck, and said I hoped things would get better – and I asked him to put out the fire. And then I left. I turned around once to look at him, a small figure squatting next to the fire, darker than all the darkness surrounding him. The next day I heard he hadn't come home.'

219

You don't wait to see whether she has more to say, you can't stay in that room any longer. You stumble out of the house, half-blind, even though escape is no longer an option. You take a few shaky steps in the snow and then collapse. Somewhere far off you can hear screaming. It takes a while before you realize you're making the sound yourself and even then you can't stop. The sound comes from elsewhere, not your body, it's just passing through, and it doesn't disappear when you finally go quiet, exhausted and smaller now.

The dog comes up to the gate, wagging its tail submissively. Now you're feeding her, she's not scared of you anymore. She even tries to lick your hand but you shoo her away and she just stands there, looking confused. You pull the door to her cage wide open, but she doesn't move.

'Go on then!' you scream. 'Get the hell out of here!'

She hesitates briefly before running off. Just for a moment, all you see is the beauty of the animal, which suddenly looks very wolf-like; strangely enough, this makes her less threatening, a wild animal and nothing more.

When you look up Hannah is standing next to you. She's standing there watching you chase away the dog, her dog, her hands hanging heavily by her sides.

'He didn't drown,' she says, 'although that may be what he died of. The cold got him long before that.'

It's quiet outside, the sounds muffled by the snow. The woods here are different: endless, and much darker than back home. Just before the party Hannah said, 'People get lost here. They go into the woods to pick berries or mushrooms and never come back. The way to avoid that is to keep shouting to each other, to call out to each other all the time.'

That's where Mark and you went wrong, you stopped calling.

You stopped even before Kito came to you, but you didn't realize it. Because he lacked for nothing, right? And there was nothing you couldn't give him, was there?

Now you walk along the edge of the forest, alone, and the life you used to lead is far away, like it was never yours to begin with. It could be a film you once saw or a book you once read, something made up. The only things that really exist are the things around you. The chill here is calm, there's no wind. You too could walk into the forest and get lost. You'd get tired and go to sleep the way they do in fairy tales. Hannah wouldn't notice you were gone until later. She could call her neighbours but where would they start looking? You'd be long dead by the time they found you, not until the spring maybe, when the snow starts melting. It's a relief to think about dying like that, to think there's always that option – even though you know it's always different in reality, dying like that isn't peaceful and the cold isn't like it's described in fairy tales. Maybe the experience of dying itself will bring you closer to him than you could ever hope to get otherwise.

Despite this, you keep skirting the edge of the forest. You don't belong to the living but you don't belong to the dead either; you're stuck here, on the edge.

Later, all those students of hers, his classmates, will talk about the boy who suddenly disappeared. As time passes, his disappearance will come to seem more important to them. By then, no one will admit to ever having picked on him; give it twenty years and they'll all claim to have been his best friend.

A crow flies up, cawing, as you approach the cemetery. The graves are covered in snow; winter makes even death almost invisible here.

You wait.

You wait for a long time, but all remains silent.

You wonder whether any of the *babas* ever come here, which of them has a husband or child lying here, finished off by alcohol and cigarettes or perhaps some stupid accident. Your own yearning is terrifying. If only someone were here now, one of those strong old women, who could put her wiry arms around you and cry with you.

You could burn the house down tonight, you worked it all out ages ago. You'd sprinkle petrol on the trunk of the old vine, hanging rags drenched in linseed oil in the branches. Then you'd set the thing alight, watching the flames spread, carefully at first, then greedily. No one would cry out. You'd watch from a distance, listening to the sounds of the fire, which would be beautiful and warm in the dark night. Soon dogs would start barking, someone would come out of one of the houses. They'd try to save her, but only when it was already too late.

You think of all those things, but only as something to hold on to. Just because you've got used to the idea that you can take revenge, that there's something left to be done.

As you walked away, she said, 'I only wanted to help him.'

Her voice was small and almost imploring, and it took a moment before you understood what she was saying.